Deep Woods Odyssey

….not your typical animal story.

Ronald Gaines

ISBN: 978-057816968-2
LCCN: 2015915278
Cover Art and Illustrations by Eliseo Santos

Papaw Publications USA

PP

Odyssey: A series of wanderings or journeys usually marked by adventures, notable experiences, and changes of fortune.

Dedicated to all who love the deep woods and the wildlife adventures found there.

"Imagination grows by exercise, and contrary to common belief, is more powerful in the mature than in the young."

W. Somerset Maugham
British Author and Playwright

Referencing map helps orient movement through the forest.

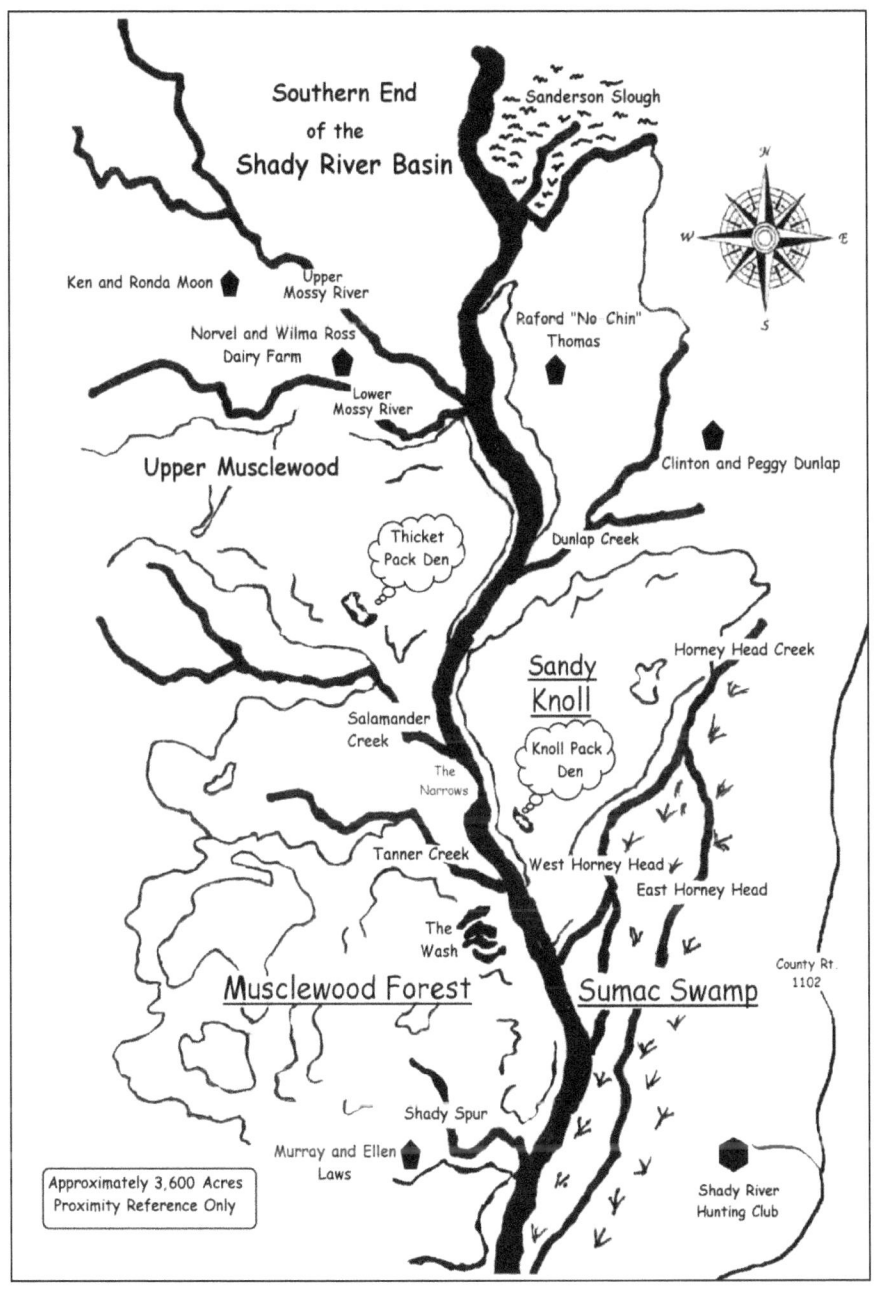

"Each species is a masterpiece, a creation assembled with extreme care and genius."

Edward O. Wilson
American Naturalist and Author

An Opening Note

The story of animals in the Shady River Basin reaches far into the past, and extends well into the modern day. The lives of mammals, large and small, birds of prey, amphibians, and reptiles of all descriptions, have long comingled in a rich and varied tapestry of experience.

However, the following pages explore only one brief snapshot in the story of Musclewood Forest wildlife. The eighteen months between the summer of 1959 and the spring of 1961, saw events which mirrored watershed developments in the Out World — the world of the Obtruders.

It was a time when valor overcame violence; devotion was more common than desertion; and the pursuit of deepened mutual understanding held the promise of a new and more hopeful future.

With the exception of bestowing upon Musclewood animals words and thoughts to which we all can better relate, the story is told in realistic, gritty terms. Evocative life and death circumstance among deep woods creatures deserves no less. .

"Sometimes I've believed as many as six impossible things before breakfast."

Lewis Carroll Author of "Alice in Wonderland"

One

Contrasting Characters

Enid paid no attention as the second of two C-133 Cargomasters made the low, noisy right turn over Sandy Knoll. In fact, he little more than raised an eyebrow.

The leader of the Knoll Pack had found a spot near the opening to his den where the sun had warmed the ground. Understandably, Enid took little notice of something he'd seen so many times before. The contrast between the uncomplicated life of deep woods creatures and Obtruder's rumpus goings-on may have nowhere been clearer than when the huge planes flew over peaceful scenes on Sandy Knoll.

One of the landing patterns at North Charleston's airport regularly provided sights and sounds to which creatures in the deep woods had become accustomed, but never fully accepted. Shrieking aircraft were just one of the obtrusive things those from the Out World forced upon the deep woods and its animal residents.

Moments earlier, the first C-133 had sent Bren hurrying to scrunch up behind his father. The most inquisitive of Enid and Bree's six-month-old pups showed only his head above his father's back as the second giant plane flew across the opening in the treetops.

Exploring a muskrat hole along the river bank was one thing, but standing up to the shrill whine of four 5,900 horsepower turbo prop engines was something else indeed.

"Father, I'm afraid of the machines," said Bren, his almond-colored eyes blending fear and dread.

Bren's father responded with a single deep breath before closing his eyes, and adjusting his head and neck slightly to the left across his front legs.

Enid was a stout and determined leader, a particularly effective hunter, a very good father, and a trustworthy defender of the Knoll Pack's territory. But he'd reached the point in life when an afternoon nap was satisfying.

"Rest now, Bren. Those machines will do us no harm."

Enid knew the Obtruders who moved upright through the woods were the ones that often came with ill-will in their hearts. Those which passed overhead in the shiny, loud machines; rode vehicles along well-worn paths through the trees, or moved up and down the river in floating metal were not the worry.

>>><<<

The year was 1960, and consequential events continued to take place in the Out World. Happenings foretold of shifts in the Obtruders' lives, some of which would please many, while others vexed millions.

An Obtruder war in a far-away place was to intensify as the leader in America ordered more fighters into the battle. It was a growing entanglement that would divide great numbers of those that dwelled in the Out World.

It was a time when the weather satellites were first positioned, giving Obtruders their first look at elements from above the swirling formations.

In order to pinpoint locations, Obtruders would power up the earliest navigational satellites, giving birth to the Global Positioning System. Soon

[3]

the warring ways of conflicted Obtruders would have the heightened terror of pinpoint accuracy.

Shortly after the year began, four young Obtruders took seats at a forbidden counter, and the signs of sweeping change were emerging in a key Out World nation's social and political order.

With the selection process in favor of one named Kennedy, the Obtruders selected their youngest leader ever, only to later see his leadership end in sudden violence and persistent accusations.

Of course, as the Out World convulsed, animal residents of the Shady River were not privy to the mega-happenings in the other world. Their life experience was confined to 3,600 acres of river drainage territory, and interactions with the furred, scaled and feathered residents which called it home.

Typically, forest animals led stable lives, free from the unpredictable, ragged, and often complicated entanglements of life in the Out World. It was when Obtruders chose to make forays into Shady River Basin that things changed.

When they came there was no way even the wisest and most perceptive animals could fully comprehend their intelligence, and the tools such intellect could devise.

Even though they didn't have the vision of the hawk, Obtruders had magic glass to overcome the disadvantage of distance.

Even though they couldn't stalk with the precision of the felines, Obtruders could study animal pathways and lay in wait, or simply place unseen jaws to do the deed. Knowing animals of the deep woods to be creatures of habit, Obtruders identified the preferred trails before setting the steel traps or suspending the biting snares.

The instruments brought from the Out World could shoo away the dark with a single click, or give birth to fire's yellow and orange dance to chill the resolve and befuddle the mind of all deep woods creatures.

Obtruders could manipulate sound to make animals follow their strongest instincts, hurrying to a place of the outsider's choosing. There they used the deadliest fruits of their intellect to knock the life out of animals overpowered by the most efficient predators of all – sojourners from the Out World.

However, it should be understood that animal residents in the Shady River Basin were quite capable in their own right. Especially true among the larger mammals, there was an innate array of cunning, adaptable skills no Obtruder could match.

Unlike the native animals, Obtruders couldn't race at dizzying speeds through the dense forest and entangling flora.

Unlike the native animals, Obtruders couldn't survey an adversary long before the adversary could survey them.

Unlike the native animals, Obtruders couldn't devise a countering strategy informed by smells that rode the wind.

And, unlike native animals, Obtruders couldn't rely upon advantages gained through a life lived entirely in the densest corners of the wild.

There was another preeminent trait in the makeup of most large, deep woods creatures which served their survival. It was an attribute fostered by experience and keen perception.

In young wild life, it appeared first as *instinct* – an unthinking, automatic response mechanism.

As the creatures' instinct matured, it evolved into what is most often called *intuition* – the ability to determine whether something is one way or another without prolonged reasoning.

As intuitive skills sharpened, they evolved into *insight* – the ability to understand a broad array of life's circumstances.

When the creatures of Shady River Basin dealt with Obtruders or any other threat in the deep woods, their ability to understand a situation immediately and accurately was essential to maximizing the odds of long life.

Collectively, insight-rich decisions became the bedrock of *deep-woods wisdom* – the supreme element in helping a great forest beast live its own odyssey to the fullest.

Two

Carolina Dogs

The Pack living on the Knoll was a striking, close-knit group. Their shapes, and with the exception of Corson and his daughter, Twill, even their coloration was unexpectedly consistent. It was not untypical for a pack of feral dogs to conduct themselves like one big family, but it was quite unusual for members to look so uniformly alike.

Consistency in the Sandy Knoll group's appearance was easily explained. The genetic pool from which they'd come was dominated by a single and ancient line of canids.

In coming from Eurasia, the Pack's ancestors used the same land bridge as North America's earliest settlers.

Enid's ancestors arrived in North America 14,000 years before the two C-133 Cargomasters flew over Sandy Knoll in the spring of 1960. They were truly an indigenous breed.

As was the case with other dogs in and around the Basin, they didn't arrive in North America on the ships of European explorers. They were in North America long before Christopher Columbus arrived in the new world.

Descendants of European dogs lived in Out World cities, towns, and homesteads along the edge of the Shady River wetlands. The fact was Enid led a Pack whose roots were far longer and older than the dogs found in the Out World.

For decades, Obtruders had called them "Swamp Dogs", "Yellow Dogs", "Indian Dogs" or "American Dingos".

In the first half of the 20th Century, nothing was known of the dogs' past, as was obviously the case with the special canids' future. What lay ahead for descendants of the Sandy Knoll Pack was at least as interesting as their storied past.

>>><<<

In fact, to fully gain perspective on the Sandy Knoll canines, it's necessary to look at their future as well as their past. In the decades following 1960, the canids were to become known as "Carolina Dogs", destined to gain full recognition in the Out World as a distinct and rare breed.

None of the residents along the river knew of the ancient cave wall paintings, where charcoal black and ochre were mixed with spit or fat and rubbed on the porous rock surface. The dogs depicted there had physical traits very much like Enid's group. In the cave art, they appeared to have tan, ginger, dark brown, black or piebald coats, just like the dogs on Sandy Knoll.

Long snouts, permanently-erect, pointed ears, athletic-looking waists, and a tail that curved back over on the dog's back were all depicted in the paintings.

The likeness was striking and undeniable.

Raford "No-Toes" Thompson, a Basin resident, avid outdoorsman, and lover of wildlife, was first in the Shady River area to speak of how much the dogs reminded him of the Australian Dingo.

He first made the comment to a member of the Shady River Hunting Club, and the comparison stuck. Locals began speaking of the "dingos" that lived in a den under a tree near the top of Sandy Knoll.

Describe them as you may, there is no question the den was occupied by truly feral dogs. They roamed freely, with no direct shelter or food intentionally supplied by Obtruders. There was no evidence of socialization within or from the outside world. They were classically, wild.

It can also be said that Enid didn't lead a pack in the strict sense of the word. His social unit was more a "group" than a "pack"....the word most often used when describing the social unit of wolves.

Wolf packs form when a male and female meet, breed, and begin to dominate a vacant territory. Members are all related to one another, held together by what might be called a blood bond, or affectional tie.

Over the years, the Sandy Knoll canines' basic social structure differed from that of the wolf, in that it featured several stable, monogamous pairs – all joining together in interdependency when hunting, caring for the young or defending territory. Pressure toward a more wolf-like, hierarchical social structure, with an alpha male, only occurred when an extraordinarily strong male stepped forth, and assumed the onus of leadership – a male such as Enid.

Three

New Neighbors down South

Partially hidden by large leathery leaves on a low-hanging limb of a southern magnolia tree, Enid was seated atop a small rise just northwest of the farmhouse near the bottom of the Basin. The homestead had been part of the Pack's southern range since long before Enid's time.

When Obtruders moved into or out of the Basin members of the Sandy Knoll Pack always took notice. "How many are there Enid?" asked

Corvin, who was lying under a limb on the other side of the sprawling tree.

"I can't tell for sure Corvin, perhaps five or six. Two look small. One is newly born."

As usual, Enid's sharp eyes served him well. Dr. Murray Laws and his wife, Ellen, were moving into the recently up-dated farm house. Rory, their 14-year-old son and Alenna, their 10-year-old daughter, were helping carry items from the pickup truck to the house. Robbie, the 18-month-old was thrilled at just being able to toddle between the back porch and the truck.

One or two members of the Pack had been checking on the place every few days since they first heard the contractor's hammers and saws. For several weeks the group had known that a new group of Obtruders was moving into the southern end of their range.

"Enid, I'm sorry to see more Obtruders moving into the old house. They are living on both ends of our range now. Our territory grows smaller."

"It's not the new Obtruders that concern me, Corvin. I'm troubled to know this will stop our work with the young at this place. It met our needs in so many ways."

With the house and two out structures empty for almost three years, the small farm had been a good place to bring Knoll Pack pups to practice hunting tactics with the mice, ground squirrels and rabbits living under the buildings.

In addition, there were three large brush piles that had been left behind when the last Obtruders moved. Those too had been a favorite place of the Carolina Dogs for training the young. But with the new family's arrival, the large brush piles, as well, would no longer be available for the Pack's use.

Even though Enid didn't sense the tenseness and threat from the new arrivals that he did among Obtruders around the Hunt Club directly across the river, he knew caution was always called for where Obtruders were concerned.

"Corvin, we'll continue to watch this group. We will study their ways and judge their intentions. Like us, they have young, which may temper aggression. Where there are young there is more caring and love," said Enid, again offering wise and measured words.

"Let's get back to the den," said Enid as he stood to retrace their route along the river toward the Knoll.

Just before Corvin joined Enid in getting to his feet, he saw movement at the back of the house.

"Wait," said Enid's closest friend among the other Knoll Pack males. "There's someone coming out. Let's wait a little longer. We may see something that tells us more of these new arrivals."

Enid spun and dropped back to the ground. Instinctively, both ferals lowered their heads.

>>><<<

After bounding through the back door, Rory and Alenna ran across the yard. Rory was chasing his younger sister, who was mixing screams with laughter, as each expressed excitement with the new home and the thick forest surroundings.

The children stopped at the edge of the woods, unaware they were standing within two hundred feet of the wild dogs. Only the Carolina Dogs' eyes moved, following every twitch made by the young Obtruders. It was a rare opportunity to observe outworlders in detail from a well-concealed hiding place.

The hardwoods, thick longleaf, eastern white pines, intertwined young oaks, black gum, and occasional palmetto tree made the woods beyond the back yard look foreboding to the uninitiated, like Alenna. The same was not the case with Rory.

"Alenna, I can't wait to explore all the way to the River. Dad grew up near here, and he says the river is clear, and the banks fall slowly to the water. There have got to be some great places to see," declared Rory, speaking resolutely with his arms crossed firmly on his chest.

[15]

"Aren't you afraid of bears, wolves or big snakes that might be out there Rory?" asked Alenna incredulously.

"No, I'm not sister. I'm gonna get to know these woods real good, and the animals that live there even better. It'll be great!"

Just as Rory finished his vow of friendship with the forest, his father called him and his sister back to the house. Their excitement wouldn't permit a direct route to the kitchen door. It was more fun to skirt the edge of the woods as they ran along the tree line around the northern edge of the yard.

Seeing them slow and walk back inside, Enid and Corvin raised their heads, and again sat up under the thick, covering magnolia.

"Come on, Corvin. Let's go," said Enid as he turned to again adopt the steady gait for which he was well known. His strides had always been a little quicker than those of the other males in the den. It reflected his overall demeanor – focused and confident.

"Enid, slow down please. I want to ask you something."

Enid slowed, turning to the right to see his trusted companion coming to a stop.

"What do you think of these new Obtruders?" Corvin was anxious to hear Enid's thoughts following their unusually close look at the two young members of the family.

"Corvin, right now I have no feelings about the newcomers. The young ones are interested in our trees. Perhaps they love them as we do, or perhaps their carelessness will bring the red and orange dance to destroy them," said Enid, turning again to look in the direction of the Laws' house.

"The young ones make happy sounds, and that's good. But we must also remember the happy sounds made by older Obtruders when one of the forest creatures lies dead at their feet."

Enid stood still for another moment, pondering his words, before turning quickly and resuming the jog-like pace north. Corvin, slightly smaller and lighter, tried to keep within a half step of the Pack's top male. It was a challenge to which he'd grown accustomed when the two moved together through the forest.

>>><<<

With the majority of the heavier move-in chores behind them, Ellen was standing in a chair putting porcelain dishes on the top shelf of the cupboard. Murray was handing his wife pieces of her mother's treasured collection.

"Murray, when are you going to start your survey trips into the forest?"

"Not for a while. I want to make sure you and the kids are comfortably settled before I start traipsing off all day. A fair amount of information is available at the state forestry department. I'll probably start in an office there, and get to the field work in a week or so.

Dr. Murray Laws was a dendrologist with the United States Forestry Service. His work required the family move from one forest ecology to another. In each location, he documented basic forest health and reproductive status of woody plants on federally-controlled woodlands.

State forestry departments often called him in to help with similar research at the state level. That was the case in the family's move to the Shady River Basin.

State funds had been authorized to remodel the house for the family's use, during what was expected to be a two-year project. University students in ecological science were to be rotated into the project to assist with field work.

On the first evening in their new home, Ellen scrambled eggs and fried smoked sausage. Toast, homemade jelly, and chunky hash browns rounded out the quick-and-easy meal.

"Rory, I saw you and your sister looking into the forest this afternoon. What do you think of this place?"

"Dad, it's great and I can't wait to explore the woods. There's got to be some fun places out there, and a lot of animals to see."

Rory's response tripped his mother's always-at-the-ready worry switch. Having moved to the Basin from suburban Pittsburg, the prospects of her children roaming in the woods, likely out of sight and beyond ear shot, had crossed Ellen's mind more than once.

"Rory, I want you to go slow in exploring the woods around here. From the maps I've seen, they are dense, and the places along Shady River must be wet and muddy. There could be quick sand back there," said his mom, as she leaned forward in her chair for added emphasis.

Murray smiled and offered some assurance. "Ellen, I'll be taking Rory and Alenna with me until they get to know the area. We're gonna go slow when it comes to that river and the Musclewood Forest wetlands. Aren't we guys?"

"Yes, we are, dad," replied Rory, while his sister smiled her wide-eyed agreement around a large bite of ketchup-covered eggs.

To further comfort his wife, Murray pressed the subject a bit.

"And you two, we're also gonna set up some boundaries back there beyond which you are not to go. And I mean you are not to go! Understand?"

Rory glanced at Alenna before looking at his father and nodding agreement. The Laws' oldest child had always displayed an adventurous streak.

The idea of boundaries limiting his exploration was no perfect cup of tea for the energetic 14-year-old.

Deer, turkey, rabbits, squirrels, ducks, skunks, chipmunks, quail, hawks, an armadillo from time to time, skittish foxes here and there, raccoons, a sleepy-eyed possum, noisy crows, and a myriad of song birds were regulars in the Musclewood – each with its own story to tell.

Rory was right. There was great variety in the wildlife to be seen and enjoyed. However, not all the animal residents would welcome the children's attention. Drawing near to some of the Musclewood Forest and Sumac Swamp's animal residents would require vigilance. Danger was there, and it was real.

As they ate that late-evening breakfast, Murray and Ellen's words of caution would have likely been spoken with more conviction, had they known what new danger was soon to be in the southern end of Sumac Swamp.

Something was coming that no creature along Shady River had seen in many decades – something that was more than a match for any of the Musclewood heavyweights.

Four

The Danger, the Dogs and the Den

After leaving the woods behind the Laws' home, Enid and Corvin followed their usual route north along the western bank of Shady River. Always mindful of not being too much in the open, they stayed fifteen to twenty yards away from the Shady River's edge.

As with most rivers in the coastal plain, the Shady was considerably wider than it was deep. Near the main flow, the high-water line was well back into the woods. The area close to the water's edge, where frequent high water had taken its toll, featured only scattered and rotting stumps.

>>><<<

Just before reaching Tanner Creek, the dogs' path took them between the river and a place known as "The Wash". The spot was dominated by large rocks where, over time, heavy rain had separated them from the surrounding soil. Several species of forest dwellers, including red wolves in times past had made their home among and below the rocks in the outcropping.

In the spring of 1960, a mated pair of red foxes was using the den to conceal their young. The family crawled along a smooth tunnel on the eastern side of the formation to access a sizable chamber under two of the largest boulders.

When they first arrived, although little work had been required, the male and his vixen spent time re-excavating parts of the den. Most of the walls had long been worn smooth by the variety of animal families that had made the rock formation their home.

Standing atop the largest boulder as the two Knoll Pack members neared, Ingrum instinctively took two quick steps toward the den entrance. Once he recognized Enid and Corvin, the fiery-red male offered a greeting.

"Enid," said Ingrum, as his bushy tail extended straight out from the top of his rump. The two had seen each other many times along the river. Only in recent months, had they begun to exchange greetings.

Under Enid's leadership, the Knoll Pack had made it clear they meant Ingrum and his family no harm. Clearly, the diminutive foxes were no threat to the burly troop on the Knoll.

"Greetings, Ingrum. I hope Pixlee and your kits are well," replied Enid as he and Corvin stood mere paces from the den entrance with no tension between themselves and the red fox.

"They are, and how is it on the Knoll among your group?"

"Our journey continues, and each day we bring our best efforts to the tasks we face," replied Enid.

"There's something I must tell you and Corvin," said the fox as he stepped toward the downward slope of the boulder and jumped to the ground. His tone and eyes reflected the burden of his message.

Just as their father was about to speak, two kits appeared in the opening to the den. "Go back in the lower chamber," snapped Ingrum, as his vixen appeared in the opening between the two youngsters.

"Pixlee, please take them back inside, and keep them there while I finish speaking with Enid and Corvin."

The Vixen promptly nuzzled the two kits back down the entranceway and into a back corner of the den. She knew what her mate was about to disclose. The news would bring fear to the hearts of every mother with young in the Musclewood.

"Enid, I saw two members of the Thicket Pack this morning. It was at a distance, but I'm sure one of them was Thorn. The other was the large red bitch dog that is always with him. I don't know her name."

Enid and Corvin turned toward one another before looking back at Ingrum. The small fox was tense, and very concerned by the news he had shared. Any small, smart canid would have been.

"Are you sure it was Thorn?" asked Corvin.

"There's no mistaking Thorn. He's back in the Musclewood!"

Corvin and Enid nodded thanks, a gesture Ingrum returned with little change in his grim expression.

The Carolina Dogs resumed their journey back to Sandy Knoll, while Ingrum reentered the den where Pixlee and the kits were waiting. The tensed vixen was still in the back corner of the chamber. Ingrum dropped down at her side.

"What was their response, Ingrum?"

"They said little. There's little to say. The monster is back, and so must be the killers that run with him. We all must move with greater caution. You and our young are not to go out of the den without me nearby," ordered Ingram, even as he fully understood his presence would make little difference should the Thicket Pack come in force.

The fright in Ingrum's home was well-founded. In the recent past, all six members of a fox family were killed by Thorn and his group, including kits only a few weeks old. Disturbingly, none of the dead foxes were eaten. It appeared they were killed simply for the killing.

>>><<<

The two Knoll veterans quickened their pace as Ingrum's alarming report swelled in their heads. With just under two hundred yards to go, they broke into a run, motivated by the agonizing thought of the Thicket Pack's return. The threat it posed for even well-established, capable family units such as the Sandy Knoll Pack was cause for genuine concern. When they drew close and saw no activity around the den entrance, both males were jolted.

"No! No, Enid! There is no movement around the tree!" shouted Corvin. To see none of the Pack members routinely active near the entrance at the base of the old live oak was rare indeed.

Finally, Seph and one of his pups emerged from the den entrance to begin the greeting Enid and Corvin expected to see.

The three males rubbed noses, offered yelps, high-pitched whines, and aggressive muzzle licking in a strong act of greeting.

As the enthusiastic actions moved from bounces to jumping on each other's back, the rambunctious antics knocked Seph's pup back onto the slope of the den entranceway. She rolled all the way to the bottom near the opening into the first of three chambers.

Little Tesha got back to her feet, only to see the three males eagerly crawling down the entrance tunnel behind her. It was all she could do to get out of the way as Enid, Corvin, and her father emerged into the spacious common area.

Always trying to stay close to the action, the five-month-old Tesha was frequently pinballed at the adults' feet. As with most young members of any species, there were differences in personalities, actions, and temperament from one offspring to the next. No other youngster was more engaging or engaged than Tesha.

Adult members regarded Tesha and her brother, Aeran, as noticeably smaller than typical five-month-olds. The collective sense of paternity within the Sandy Knoll Pack intensified when it came to the well-being of pups, especially those seeming needful of extra protection and care.

It was that most basic sense of shared responsibility which brought Bree, Enid's mate, hurrying to check on Tesha when she first came rolling down the entrance tunnel.

Bree pressed her nose against Tesha's back, as the small female came to a stop. She was attempting to steady the awkwardly-tumbling pup, as well as sniff out any possible injury.

Not until she made sure Tesha was unhurt did Bree move back to her own litter. As Bree stepped away, Bedwyr was there to take her place. Tesha's mother had been in a back area when her daughter tumbled backwards down the entrance tunnel.

A contributing factor in the Carolina Dog community's attentiveness toward Seph and Bedwyr's pups was the recent loss the couple had suffered.

Originally, there were four pups in Seph and Bedwyr's litter. One, a male, died shortly after birth. The other, a female at about five weeks, managed to elude her mother's eye just before dawn. Tesha's sister worked her way up the tunnel to the outside. She was never seen again. The Pack's best efforts failed to find her or discover any clue as to what her fate might have been.

Only one deep woods resident knew what happened to the little female pup, and thus far he had chosen not to share what he knew of the female pup's fate.

At the beginning of the 1960's, the Sandy Knoll Pack's makeup was simple, but sound. There were five fully-grown males: Enid, Corvin, Seph, Captain, and Corvin's half brother, Mace.

The previous fall, Corvin and Mace's mother was killed by a shot from the passenger window of a passing dump truck on State Route 1102. She dropped in her tracks at the edge of the woods.

Their father, Roush, left the group shortly after the loss of his mate and never returned. Mace, fifteen months younger than Corvin, entered a difficult period after losing both parents. He became very much a loner, never taking a mate, and engaging only in limited interaction with most Pack members.

That spring, the group's alpha pair, Enid and Bree, was raising four six-month-old pups – Bren and Banner, males, and two females, Modred and Castle.

Corvin, and his mate, Gaius, had known only partial success in delivering their first and only litter of pups. In their fourteenth month, Gwain and Twill were in good health; routinely making meaningful contributions toward meeting the group's hunting efforts. Corvin and Gaius' third pup never managed its first breath after Gaius delivered at dawn on a Sunday morning in early March of 1959.

Whether it was a matter of ultimate protection, hygiene in the den, removal of a smell that might attract any number of hungry predators or simple nutrition, the pup was eaten, along with the afterbirth.

>>><<<

In considering life among the Carolina Dogs, it's not just the Pack's history, social structure, potential threats and instinctual practices that should be considered; there was also the intriguing physical configuration of the den itself. The Pack's home was exceptional in the most basic way. There was simply nothing else like it in the entire Shady River Basin.

The dirt around roots of a large live oak had been excavated, and the huge root system lay exposed in a dome-like structure across the top and down the sides. The unusual, hcmispherical root configuration spanned an area seven feet across. The chambers were thirty-six inches high in most places, requiring little to no crouch as the larger animals moved about.

One feature bore witness to the many years it served the needs of canids. In places, deep gouges could be seen where growing pups had gnawed on the live oak's roots at the point where they reentered the dirt floor.

Recently opened bites and scrapes blended with much older scars. It wasn't difficult to picture a pup chewing away, while waiting for adults to return from a hunt.

The two back rooms opened diagonally off the front, primary-gathering area. Both were used for sleeping, with no apparent room assignment within the group.

However, when it came to chamber usage, there was one exception. The room that had been excavated on the right served as a birthing chamber. It was used exclusively by the expectant male and female until the newborns were a few weeks old.

Technically, there was a third space off the front chamber. It appeared little more than an afterthought – a broad, shallow indentation in the dirt wall behind two of the larger, fully-exposed live oak roots on the east side of the front room.

The spot was used mostly as a retreat for pups who had incurred the wrath of one or both parents. Requiring a pup enter from the side between the roots and chamber wall, it was a great place to lay and peek out between the tree's reddish-brown legs, while hoping to play on the sympathy of the scolding parents.

Finally, there was something almost surreal – natural lighting. Digging between roots on the surface had resulted in several openings where sun or moonlight could reach the den floor. It was a unique place, home to a unique group of canids.

Five

A Strategy Session

Following a meal consisting of several muskrats, two squirrels and a large rabbit, the Knoll Pack settled in for the evening. During the day, Enid and Corvin had made no mention of the Thicket Pack's return.

All the older dogs were aware of what the renegade band had done the previous year. Violent attacks were inflicted on all manner of forest dwellers, with both wild and domestic animals falling victim.

Then, with the death of two Pack members at the hand of armed Obtruders, the violence from the thicket in the Upper Musclewood abruptly ended.

Wilma Ross, as good a shot as her husband had ever been, took down one of the newest Thicket Pack members as the marauders chased a calf in the upper pasture at Ross Dairy.

The second dog killed just before the Thicket Pack disappeared was Kasbon, Thorn's heir apparent. A member of the Shady River Hunting Club killed the shaggy black dog as it crossed the back side of the Club's property near the shooting range. Showing the early stages of mange, Kasbon was an exceptionally rough-looking character, but strong and particularly vicious.

Some deep woods animals thought losing the two Pack members prompted the Thicket Pack's movement northward. Whatever the details leading up to the exodus, at least a portion of the group had returned.

Only recently had animals in the Musclewood begun to resume their lives without feeling as though they must continually be tense and watchful. If Ingrum was right, and he likely was, the tension and terror would surely begin again.

An hour before dawn on the morning after Ingrum's announcement, Enid got up and made his way out of the den, steeping around Bree, Captain, Corvin and Gaius, along with Corvin's two 14-month-old pups, all of whom were sleeping in the front chamber. Unknown to Enid, Mace had left the den thirty minutes earlier.

Enid had just sat down outside the entrance when Corvin came out of the den into the bright moonlight. He walked around Enid, and stood to the right of the group's leader.

"There was no sleep for me as well," whispered Corvin, maintaining his stare down the front slope of the Knoll.

Enid turned his head slowly to the right, and looked at his good friend. "Do you think he's taken them back to their former home in the Upper Musclewood?"

"It's likely. The position is easily defended. The sides and back are protected by the rock formation. They were able to turn away our attacks before," answered Corvin, offering a reasoned answer to a question he'd already considered.

"When do we tell the others?" asked Corvin, as he turned toward Enid, anticipating Enid's answer to a central and obvious question.

>>><<<

There was no doubt about what lay ahead. From the moment all the Pack knew of the rekindled danger, life in and around the den would again succumb to fearful pressure.

The ferals from the thicket enjoyed a physical advantage. While the typical Carolina Dog weighed 40 to 60 pounds, the Thicket Pack ferals were mixed breeds, weighing as much as 100 pounds. In the past, there had always been two or three members that weighed 100 pounds, or more. Carolina Dogs stood 24 to 28 inches at the shoulder, while in many cases Thicket Pack members stood 30 to 36-inches high.

The size advantage had been decisive in confrontations the previous year. Several Sandy Knoll members were badly mauled. Tragically, a spirited and bright-eyed 9-month-old female died from her injuries.

"We will tell them when the light comes, and we all can be together. I think it's important each knows before another day begins. I'm going to tell them before we hunt," said Enid, as he lifted his head into the cool breeze to claim any message a smell might bring.

"Should we go in force to hunt, leaving our females and young exposed?" asked Corvin, knowing it was likely Enid had already given the question thought.

Corvin felt he never broached an important subject Enid hadn't, to some degree, already considered. Even to a smart, realistic thinker like Corvin, strategizing with Enid and his one-step-ahead skills proved irritating at times.

"Only Mace, you and I will hunt in the early light. Captain and Seph will stay at the den. We will move carefully, doing what must be done. We will go to the swamp, and take young hogs for our families."

"You prefer that plan over going to the herder's land for goats?" asked Corvin. The black and white Carolina Dog couched his question in the realization that goats didn't have five-inch tusks like the giant demon hog of the Sumac.

Corvin was thinking about the last time the Knoll Pack stalked the swamp, relying more on an aggressive hunt and direct confrontation than chance encounter at the outskirts of the notorious hog's territory.

The Sandy Knoll dogs knew the huge rust-colored boar with the irregular black markings was more than capable of dealing with feral dogs that ventured into the swamp.

All experienced creatures in and near the Sumac knew the strength and threat that was Wartek.

"If we fail, Captain, Seph, Gaius, Gwain and Twill will go to the herder's place when we return," replied Enid.

>>><<<

Just as Enid finished setting the alternate hunt, Mace rounded the massive live oak atop the den.

Corvin and Enid spun in his direction, Enid bearing teeth, and issuing a warning growl. Corvin's accompanying snarl further evidenced just how edgy the two males were. Mace jerked to a quick stop – his reaction more surprise than a countering aggression.

"Wait," said Mace, holding his head and shoulders in a strained, withdrawn position. "Please forgive my thoughtless approach, and the fright it caused!"

Over the past half hour, Mace had undertaken his own patrol of the area around the den. A light sleeper, Corvin's brother often patrolled the den's immediate perimeter at times when other predators or Obtruders might choose to threaten the Pack.

It was several moments before things settled down, and the three dogs' discussion turned to the overriding issue at hand – the return of their strongest and most threatening rivals.

As he was told of Ingrum's warning, Mace's head began to drop. His eyes fell to the 5-inch gray disfigurement down the front of his right foreleg. The leathered, crusty-looking scar was the result of his last encounter with the ferals across Shady River.

He could recall the fight clearly. Gwenfar, Thorn's rangy, rusty-red female, attacked him from a blind spot to his right, ripping and tearing at the tendons and bone just above his right front paw. The tugging bite left the ankle stiff, and the foot twisted oddly to the left.

Almost always subdued in his manner, Mace stood still, before slowly turning his head to the left, and focusing on one of the many snout pits around the den. Pregnant females routinely dug the rounded pits into which they stuck their head and nose. Perhaps to obtain some type of mineral nourishment, it was a practice peculiar to the Knoll Pack breed. Mace had seen hundreds of the bowl-shaped diggings. He was in thought, staring blankly, more than looking.

"Where have they been, and what has brought them back, Enid?" asked Mace, still focusing his day-dream-like gaze on the perfectly-round snout pit.

"I have no answer to those questions, Mace. It's important we give thought to what is before us, not Thorn's movements while away from us. They are back, and we must put all in our den on notice."

>>><<<

Shortly after dawn, Pack members gathered to hear Enid's words of warning and instruction.

"There will always be adults around the den. No hunts shall begin with less than three hunters. We hunt with clear objectives – no free-ranging. We go to the prey! We kill the prey! We gather it up, and we return to the Knoll."

Bree, standing close to her mate, thought of the most frightening incident associated with Thorn's group. The experience was on every mother's mind gathered beneath the bazaar, disordered limbs of the gigantic live oak.

Looking at Bren and Banner tumbling in the pine needles nearby, Bree addressed her mate, and indirectly the group. "The last time they were here, our home was attacked. What are we to do if that happens again? Enid, you and I must be deeply concerned, our litter is the youngest and the most at risk!"

"Bree, there are more of us this time, and the young ones are larger and stronger than last time. I will be between Thorn's group and our home," said Enid.

His vow was echoed by other males. The commitment to protect Pack members and their home was Pack-wide and firm.

[38]

Should conflict with the Ticket Pack come, it would need to be.

There were no further words among the Carolina Dogs – only silent looks exchanged as the group broke up and headed back underground – all but Enid, Corvin, and Mace.

That trio turned in the direction of the swamp in pursuit young hogs to fill empty stomachs.

Six

Studying and Stalking Sumac Hogs

Based purely on proximity, the Carolina Dogs hunted the upper end of Sumac Swamp more frequently than the lower. Regardless of the end selected, hunting Sumac terrain required a specialized combination of determination and refined technique.

Beginning where Horney Head Creek splits into its eastern and western flows, the Pack typically positioned members on the outside of each branch, and another Pack member between the branches in hopes of intercepting prey that tried to flee across the hammock.

The Carolina Dogs employed both ambush and relentless pursuit strategies in their hunts, whether the hunts were wet or dry. Pursuit was employed most often due to the Pack's great stamina. They would simply flush and run down their prey, only periodically using head-them-off tactics. Once downed, powerful, ripping jaws were used to dispatch the victim. In the moments before death came, the prey was simply eaten alive.

When hunting, predators in the Sumac most often dealt with shallow wetlands, rather than a true swamp. There was plenty of standing water, but there were also sizable patches of little more than soggy sand. Most dangerous were the muskegs – deep holes filled with water and decaying greenery in varying stages of decomposition.

Hammocks, some no more than a few inches above the surrounding water, were home to a variety of trees – broad leaf hardwoods and conifers principle among them. The contrasting ecosystems served to produce a compelling environment, as though two giant hands of terrain cards had shuffled, randomizing the wet and the dry.

The Sumac Swamp and the smaller Sanderson Slough further north, were places greatly favored by wild hogs. Whether rooting for nuts and insects, cooling off in the shallows, or simply rolling in the wet sandy mud, hogs of all ages exploited the satisfying environs for comfort and seclusion.

>>><<<

The wild hogs being sought by the three Knoll Pack members didn't operate within a refined, predictable social unit. There was no wolf-like hierarchy nor monogamous affiliation of stable, mating pairs, as was the case on the Knoll.

For many years, it had been known wild hogs demonstrated the highest reproductive rate of any large mammal. It was their prolific reproduction and patchwork mating patterns which led to a simple amalgam of individuals and little to no extended, stable affiliations.

Of course Sumac hogs, as was the case with all wild hogs, contained sounders – family groups made up of sows related over several generations and their most recent offspring.

There was also the tendency for females to seek and follow the movement patterns of large, mature boars, but any sustained familial bonding beyond the first eight to ten months between a mother and young was very sketchy, at best.

>>><<<

In 1960, there was one constant within the Sumac Swamp's wild hog population – the unquestioned alpha status of Wartek. He looked to be some sort of throwback to the menacing-looking European boars first brought to America. The long head, crooked snout, very impressive tusks, the ridge of straight coarse hair along the backbone, and almost five hundred pounds of muscled-up bulk, combined to continually restate his fearsome reputation. He was always listening, looking, and scenting the air should others enter the wooded wetlands he considered his.

On that chilly late March morning, as the Knoll threesome began their hunt, Wartek was rooting for insects and tubers in one of his favorite spots – the small triangular hammock across Shady River from The Wash. Bordered by water on all sides, it was a place where he felt unthreatened.

That day the top Sumac boar was accompanied by a sow and five squeakers, all

[42]

grubbing noisily. He was unaware of the stalk heading south down Horney Head Creek – a situation that would soon change.

Enid had begun to work his way southward just outside the Horney Head's eastern run, while Mace had entered the hammock where the west and east runs divide. Corvin was paralleling Enid's path on the outside of the western run.

Mace was the first to see the sow and shoats crossing the hammock heading toward Corvin. There was no initiating bark, yelp, or growl as Mace accelerated to the extent his stiffened ankle would permit. The chase was on.

Corvin heard the hogs coming, and began running east in hopes of heading off Mace's pursuit before the sow and shoats crossed the creek and turned south.

His timing was perfect.

As Corvin sprinted toward the creek, the sow was just getting to the gradual slope of the sandy bank. As she finished the crossing, she initiated a turn to the left in an attempt to outmaneuver the charging feral coming from the right.

Corvin knew wild hogs were not only quicker than most might expect, but faster as well. They were able to turn and accelerate mid-chase as effectively as any feral. Two or three ticks of miscalculation, and the prey would disappear into the woods, escaping the trap Corvin and Mace had in mind.

It was not the 150-pound female Corvin was targeting. He was focused on the male shoat running right behind. Both of the young hogs were struggling in the almost-chest-deep water, trying to keep their chest high as they drove forward.

Even with the hindrance of a bum ankle, Mace was closing from behind. Corvin slammed into the young hog, sinking his teeth into the male's right jowl. The commotion gave the second shoat pause – just what Mace needed to reach the young female's right flank.

Corvin's half-brother clamped down hard, while driving all four paws into the sand in a successful attempt to slow the panicked hog.

Even for well-conditioned hunters like Mace and Corvin, a 40-pound, panicked shoat proved a load – squirming, biting, and holding forth with ear-splitting squeals. Both young hogs were close to escape when Enid arrived. His head-shaking bite into the left side of the female's throat quickly turned things in Mace's favor.

With Enid jerking and tearing on the left, Mace was able to move his attack from the right hip up to the side of the female's neck. Just at the water's edge, with Enid and Mace ripping on each side of her throat, the female went to the ground. She didn't get up again.

Meanwhile, Corvin had managed to put the male on its side, and stop much of its violent thrashing. With the female stilled and close to death, Enid hurried to help Corvin finish killing the male.

From start to finish, it had taken the three dogs just over five minutes to kill both thick-skinned hogs.

Before finally escaping into the trees, the sow returned only once in a clearly dispirited attempt to repel the Carolina Dogs. Both the pursuit and the kill had been efficient. No time was wasted, as the meat was torn from the bones. There was good reason for the ferals to be about the business of leaving the dreaded boar's territory.

>>><<<

It was the squealing that drew Wartek toward the site of the assault. When it came to attacks on the smaller and younger, Wartek's interest was always based more on a possible territorial violation than some protector-of-the-species instinct or paternal impulse.

His sense of "my turf" was far more entrenched than with other boars, most of which would readily relinquish a favorite spot when threatened. Had you followed him over the course of a week, you would have seen the brute conducting business as though the entire wetlands were exclusively his domain.

Enid, Corvin, and Mace devoured all the flesh they could hold. Once swallowed, the muscle meat and organs would be transported back to the den, where it would be regurgitated and shared with the group. As was frequently the case, what remained on the two carcasses would be dragged back to the Knoll as well.

"Fill your stomachs quickly," said Enid, trying to consume his share, while looking southward in the direction from which he felt Wartek would come.

Looking up frequently from the partially-eaten hog, Corvin still had a clear vision of the pre-dawn charge into the middle of a Sandy Knoll kill, where Wartek snatched what remained of a mid-sized doe.

During that assault, Captain suffered a nasty wound in his left shoulder from Wartek's tusk. The giant boar had been quite in his approach. Almost cat-like, Wartek picked up the remains in his mouth, and moved it away from the kill site to be devoured at *his* leisure in a place of *his* choosing. All three dogs' minds were on the fearless hog, not on the successful kill, or the chunks of meat each tossed back toward their gullet.

The sow and squeakers that had been foraging with Wartek ran behind the beast for over a hundred yards. He was far too fast, as he powered in the direction of the hysterical squeals.

As he neared the scene and slowed his approach, things had grown silent. But he didn't need further noise to inform his response. He would rely on his sense of smell, which was more precise than his sight or hearing – keener even than that of a whitetail. The long snout filtered the air, and took him to the location of the intrusion.

With a sizable portion of the shoats traveling in the dogs' stomachs, Enid established a gallop-like pace, while Mace and Corvin drug the two remains. The significantly-denuded skeletal frames slid easily over the leaves and pine needles.

Enid, Mace, and Corvin had already put distance between themselves and the site of the attack when Wartek arrived. The boar found only fleshy scraps and shards of bone where the yearlings had been killed.

Envisioning what had happened; Wartek stood a moment, and looked up the west run of the creek.

I know this scent. I know who you are, and what has been done here. We will surely meet again, and I will remember.

Wartek turned and started back toward the middle of the Sumac, his tail standing straight up, with the wiry tuft of hair at its tip swaying left and right.

There was a cocksure air in Wartek's movement, a refined arrogance in the erectness in his neck, as his huge head rode the side-to-side motion of his strut.

>>><<<

With good fortune coming so early in the hunt, Enid, Corvin, and Mace had only a short distance to cover in returning to the den. The serpentine trail through the woods between the northern end of Sumac Swamp and Sandy Knoll was a byway they had traveled many times.

Following a short distance, Mace noticed movement at the water's edge. He trotted past the place where his mates made the right turn into the woods, heading directly for the den.

Mace moved on up the creek, where he found a strange scene. A large cottonmouth moccasin was struggling to swallow a substantial catfish.

It was the white bellies rolling over under the surface that had caught Mace's eye. Corvin's half-brother pawed at the serpent several times before managing to snag the snake and pull it up on the bank.

The moccasin's problem was obvious. He had swallowed the catfish down to the dorsal and pectoral fins, which in its death throes the catfish had locked in place.

The reptile couldn't walk its jaws further down the fish's body, nor could it extract its fangs to back away from the prey. It was a real-life lesson in the dangers of biting off more than one can chew or swallow.

On the bank, the snake rolled the catfish only once before Mace clamped down behind its head, and began the whipping motion he'd employed many times to kill snakes. Several poundings on the hard-packed ground, followed by two against a jagged stump, and the exhausted snake went limp. The catfish drug the ground as Mace headed for the den with the 4-foot moccasin draped across his lower jaw. The nutritious white meat proved a welcomed addition to the menu.

Seven

Thorn's Heritage

To fully understand Thorn's consistently foul temperament, one would need to go back over a decade. The year was 1948. That's when his father, Korson, was driven from under the front porch of the two-over-two farmhouse with the chalky slate siding – the house occupied by Kenneth and Rhonda Moon in 1960.

The owner at the time, Harlan Stancil, could hardly afford to keep his family fed, much less a large, almost pure-bred Rottweiler with an appetite growing faster than its feet.

On the day life with the Stancil household came to an end, Korson was nearing starvation. Over the previous four days, he'd eaten nothing but some putrid garbage and a few small rodents. He was very weak and very confused.

Why are scraps no longer being thrown into the yard? Why have stomps and shouts on the back porch replaced food and water?

Korson was only 15-months-old, and facing the harsh reality that the Obtruders wanted him gone.

"You get out from under there! Get! Get gone now!" shouted Stancil as he used the heavy wooden handle to gouge at the recoiling dog's left side.

Sharp jabs in the hip, neck, and jaw finally drove Korson from under one end of the porch. As he bolted to escape, his head and front legs became entangled in the rusty remains of chicken wire Stancil had nailed up several years earlier to keep varmints out from under the porch.

Unable to free himself, he incurred the wrath of a man enraged as much by hard times and hard luck, as by the expectations of a large, slightly clumsy, and always-hungry pup.

Trapped in the wire, the terrible lashes with the heavy harness strap, and licks from the hand-carved hoe handle became forever intertwined with the image of Obtruders and their violent ways.

Stancil fully intended to see the youngster disappear into the Upper Musclewood Forest. If that objective required broken bones and bloody gashes, so be it!

Stancil's wife on two occasions asked her husband why he didn't just shoot the dog. His answer conveyed a sort of twisted logic.

"I ain't gonna waste no bullet. Besides I don't think I could bring myself to do something like that."

The final lick with the handle cracked two of Korson's ribs. One of his eyes was swollen shut as he finally freed himself from the wire's cutting entanglement.

Violently expelled from the Stancil farm, hungry and in terrible pain, he began to nurture a burning resentment for Obtruders, and all associated with them. He was struggling to live on small rodents, random carrion, frogs, grubs, grasshoppers, and other insects. All were obtained while struggling with fierce pain. Thorn's father would never understand nor overcome his indignation, following the unprovoked violence he experienced at the hands of Harlan Stancil.

Why would he do that? I cared for him and felt he cared for me. Only anger, only hatred, only evil could do this! Obtruders! They are my enemy!

>>><<<

Such thoughts became the basis upon which Korson developed his broader view of the world – a view that came to be deeply instilled in the minds of his followers, expressly his offspring.

He passed on white-hot anger and intolerance to his son. He bequeathed a template of terror and aggression, not only toward Obtruders, but toward most living things in the Shady River Basin.

Shortly after Thorn's birth, Korson's feelings became even more jaundiced when his mate, Queen, tragically stepped into the steel jaws of an Obtruder's trap.

When Korson found where the trap had done its work, he also saw that Queen's lower right shoulder and leg had been chopped off, and placed back in the trap as a singularly morbid bait option.

After the death of Queen, Korson and Thorn increased their efforts at taking the Obtruders' farm animals and yard pets. In addition to violence directed toward the Obtruders, the Thicket Pack assaulted other deep woods animals, ravaging their dens, commandeering their kills, not eating but killing their young, and leaving many animal families devastated.

>>><<<

Korson's death came as he had lived – violently!

On a Friday in mid-November, 1948, he led the Thicket Pack into an Obtruder hunting camp.

[53]

The smell of pan-fried steak pulled the hungry ferals from their hiding place in a nearby gulley. Several pieces of uncooked venison lying on a drink box were the primary targets.

The ferals came in quickly, seeking to confound and intimidate the Obtruders. If successful, the strategy of surprise and confusion would permit time to snatch the food, and disappear back into the protective cover of the Upper Musclewood.

The three men's reaction was more organized, and much angrier than Korson had expected. The confrontation quickly became one-on-one. The oldest hunter's leg was badly torn, and one of his companions was bitten several times on the left forearm. Even though they were momentarily confused and frightened, the Obtruders managed to stand their ground.

There is no question the sharp hunger pangs were strong motivation for Korson, Thorn, and the other pariahs. Even though it was highly motivated, and perhaps understandable, the frontal challenge of armed Obtruders in the middle of their camp proved Korson's most brazen and costly act.

Two of the Pack members were killed by pistol shots where they fought. Raspin, Korson's heir apparent to the leadership spot, died instantly. His jaws were still locked on the left forearm of the man who used the revolver in his right hand to blast a hole through the big yellow dog's neck.

Most often, Korson was thoughtful in such actions. But the camp attack, too risky and too rushed, turned out to be profoundly wrong. The thoughtful anticipation Korson so often displayed was clouded by overconfidence and disregard for the threat posed by armed hunters. Three strong, productive adult males in the Thicket Pack died, including Korson.

Charging northward into the Upper Musclewood, blood was spattering on Thorn's face as the 13-month-old ran behind his father. The young Rottweiler wasn't fully aware of what had happened. He knew things hadn't gone as expected, and he understood something was terribly wrong. Korson began to slow, tripping twice, before awkwardly managing to regain his balance each time.

The single shot fired by the third hunter found Korson's left side, just behind the ribcage. The .204 slug had ripped through the gut, leaving a super-heated tube of pulverized tissue.

The group was within a hundred yards of the den when Thorn's father stumbled to a stop, and collapsed under a pine recently jackknifed by a bolt of lightning.

The few remaining green needles on the tree were near death, as was the mortally-wounded leader of the Musclewood's Thicket Pack.

As one leadership term faded, another was about to begin. "Come close to me," whispered Korson. The message that formed in his mind was for Thorn only. His son would be charged with fashioning words and actions to communicate his father's final thoughts to the entire Pack.

The frightened pup lowered his frame to the ground, and began slowly dragging himself closer. Thorn was young and inexperienced, but he knew the moment would be one like few others in his life. He trembled physically and mentally.

The dying Korson spoke with preciseness in his tone.

"Hear this Thorn. You must be vigilant and always positioned to strike first. With Obtruders and forest competitors that would do us harm, there can be no trust extended."

Following a shallow breath and a reflexive series of coughs which sprayed bloody-drool onto the ground, the end was at hand.

With that final breath, Korson offered one last counsel: "Insure your caution does not dull your courage....to live long....you must always live strong."

"Please, don't leave me, father," whispered Thorn, each soft word tinged with panic.

In the winter of 1957, Korson lay dead under the charred pine. The tree seemed an appropriate marker, with its splintered trunk, drying bark, and stiffened branches.

Thorn's lasting memory of his father's face would be the strangely drawn, still-twitching upper lip. It was almost as if Korson wanted one final time to display his canines as an exclamation point to his fearsome life.

The old Rottweiler's final expression was one of anger and aggression – one he'd shown Obtruders and other deep woods adversaries most of his life.

Thorn had never felt more frightened and alone. There was no escaping the feeling his father had issued a final directive for Thorn's pending role as leader.

The 13-month-old's ascension to the top was to prove filled with challenge. He would need to quickly assume the leadership role, even as he was still defining the Pack's strategy for maintaining its power-player position in the Shady River Basin.

The loss of three strong males in the ill-fated hunter camp attack had dealt another difficult reality. Overnight, the Thicket Pack had become no more than a marginal presence in the Basin's predatory pecking order. In the instant it takes to engage a trigger, the Obtruders had relegated the Musclewood's most threatening canine troop to second-class status.

Thicket Pack Make-Up in November, 1957

Korson – Adult Male Killed in Hunting Camp Raid
Raspin – Adult Male Killed in Hunting Camp Raid
Paladin – Adult Male Killed in Hunting Camp Raid
Thorn – 13 month-old male
Gwenfar – 15 month-old female
Maston – 6 year-old male
Nester – 12 year-old male
(No pups at the time of Hunter's Camp Killings)

The preeminent question was clear: who would lead them back to the prominence they would likely lose?

There was the youngster, Thorn, and his mate, Gwenfar, only two months older.

Then there was Maston, a strong male to be sure, but one more interested in scheming and shallow, self-promotion than the difficult tasks of hunting and defending the Pack's territory.

Nester was a consideration, but just barely. He was almost deaf, and had only recently come to the Upper Musclewood from a neighboring county.

Two questionable males and two 1-year-olds could hardly be called a strong predatory group – certainly not a presence to be feared and respected by competing groups and the Basin's most sizable prey.

Whether it was one of the older males or Thorn, the post-adolescent youngster, the canid to emerge would have to be effective in decision-making and efficient in executing a Pack plan.

As Korson's son, Thorn's position was that of the obvious choice. But there would be much more involved in successfully filling the group's top position than just being Korson's son.

Thorn would have to inspire confidence, and develop great skill in situational leadership. The group's future was at stake.

Eight

Tying Up Loose Ends

Between the winter of 1957 and spring of 1960, more positives than negatives came the way of the Thicket Pack. An early positive was Thorn's speedy maturation. He was a quick study, gaining keen insight as he dealt with a variety of steps on the ladder to the top spot.

>>><<<

Shortly after filling the vacuum created by Korson's death, Thorn, on just his second attempt, drove a particularly ornery black bear from Rock Cave. It was an impressive feat for so young a feral leader, and others in the group were greatly impressed.

Really nothing more than a deeply hollowed-out area under a very old monolith, the protection it afforded from rear assaults or attacks from either side made it easy to defend.

Also, nature's version of heating and cooling helped make Rock Cave a special place. In the winter, warmth was available well into the night from the day's sunshine on the dark stone. And in the summer, the underside of the rock and the ground below was noticeably cooler than the surroundings during the hottest part of the day.

At one time, Thorn's grandfather and other Thicket Pack members had raised families at Rock Cave. Korson and Thorn's mothers were born there. Without doubt, recouping the rock formation was a contributing factor in the Pack's growing confidence in Thorn's leadership.

Improving the Thicket Pack's chemistry was also addressed by the new leader following Korson's death. For a feral social unit to be healthy, it needed several breeding pairs with four to six protective, hunting males. That was something Thorn fully understood.

>>><<<

By 1960, no litter had resulted from Thorn and Gwenfar's relationship. Given the amount of time and effort, there would likely be none.

Nolton, a Pack member that grew up in the southeastern corner of Georgia had never mated.

The large feral with the lion-like coat was a very capable hunter, especially when it came to deer. His particularly keen sense of smell and strong protective instincts contributed greatly to the Pack's overall welfare.

Chesman, Gwenfar's brother, was not a major player in any sense of the word. He was however, paired up with an impressive second-generation spaniel named Izepha. Looking more pure-bred than other Pack members, the white and black female had quickly adjusted to life in the deep woods.

Izepha roamed the middle and lower Basin with her father before coming to live with the Thicket Pack. Their owners had chosen to no longer bother with feeding the pair. As with Harlan Stancil and Korson, no bullets were wasted. Pitching them from the bed of a moving pickup was more their owners' style.

Izepha's father bounced into the path of an oncoming car and was killed instantly. Izepha managed to jump rather than be thrown. She hit more or less on her feet, and rolled to a thoroughly shaken, but unbroken stop.

In 1958, following Nester's death from an infestation of heartworms, Thorn had become more receptive to the idea of Nolton joining the Thicket Pack. For several months, had been staying as close to the den as the Pack would permit.

[62]

Nolton's final acceptance came after inviting him on a night hunt, where he proved his worth by tracking and taking the lead in bringing down a fully-grown wild boar. At the time, all Pack members were hungry, following several days of failed hunts. Nolton's successful effort was showcased by the group's empty stomachs.

"That was well done Nolton. Our Pack has benefited from your strength," said Thorn, after watching Nolton succeed in dispatching the hog. Thorn offered sniffs and muzzle nudges, signaling Nolton's admission into the Pack's ranks. Nolton would take Nester's place

The final male added to the group by Thorn between 1957 and 1960 was a muscular and aggressive canine named Wiston. Looking more like a German shepherd than any other breed, he was a migrant that had worked his way south from the Sand Hills area of South Carolina. Wiston's entire previous group had died after eating booby-trapped meat.

Wiston's former coterie made a habit of eating from a dumpster at a very upscale country Club. Following the failure of loud yells, thrown rocks, and even a gunshot or two, one of the junior chefs decided a more devious approach was in order.

The sadist used a large socket wrench to crush three soft drink bottles. Then he rolled three pounds of hamburger in the shards before tossing the lethal meal into the grass beside the dumpster.

Death came very slowly. All four of Wiston's cohorts took days to succumb, suffering greatly as the brown, digested blood hardened around their nostrils and mouths.

Only Wiston was absent when the group devoured the chef's specially-prepared, slow-death entrée.

Thorn, demonstrating leadership qualities at an early age; reclaiming the Pack's traditional home; and adding new Pack members that were difference-makers served to stabilize the group.

However, even with the several positive developments, there was another lingering issue which required Thorn's attention. It was the always-steady Nolton that chose to broach the subject.

>>><<<

"Thorn, your strengths have become the Pack's strengths," said Nolton as he lay down beside the third generation feral atop the great rock.

"All of us know your thoughts and planning are clear. Reclaiming the home of our ancestors is pleasing to us all. This is where we should be. Your ways in finding and directing new members is also a continual strength for our group," continued Nolton. Thorn's eyes remained focused on the gentle slope leading down to the small creek about fifty yards in front of Rock Cave.

"But there's one thing that remains. It resists your leadership, and creates a degree of unrest in the Pack," said Nolton, turning for the first time to look directly at Thorn.

With no responding turn, Thorn simply replied, "And what would that bc, Nolton?"

It was a question to which Thorn already had the answer – an issue which dwelled in his mind each day.

"I'm speaking of Maston's intent to challenge your leadership, and take over the Pack. As you probably know, it's not just the Pack he desires; he wishes to assume your relationship with Gwenfar."

'Nolton, I will deal with this when the time comes. It's something of which I am very aware. Maston's planning is weak, and his timing is weaker. Even if he strikes first, I will strike last."

>>><<<

The day to resolve the issue of Maston's planned coup came sooner than either Thorn or Nolton expected. It was early on a January morning in 1958, when Maston made a brash and seemingly spontaneous attempt to overthrow Thorn.

At 2-years-old, Thorn was already taller, thicker, and stronger than his father had been at the time of his death.

[65]

Maston's effort was ill-conceived and likely doomed to failure from the very beginning.

While Thorn was sleeping just under the front edge of the sheltering monolith, Maston attacked the back of Thorn's shoulder. The assault was sudden and savage, numbing Thorn's s•••houlders and front legs. Maston used his strong neck and shoulder muscles to wrench his head from side to side. Thorn came close to losing consciousness. Finally, he managed to roll over, pulling Maston across his body to the ground on the opposite side.

Thorn continued to roll, forcing his attacker's teeth through and out of the flesh along his back.

The enraged Rottweiler got to his feet, spun to his left, and sank his teeth into Maston's chest just below the neck. He tore into the hound, rapidly shaking his head as he positioned his left leg across his challenger's chest. He then used his upper body strength, pinning his attacker.

A flash of panic awash in a flood of adrenaline helped Maston raise his head enough to bite deeply into Thorn's muzzle.

As with the bite to the back of his neck, the brown, mixed-breed Rottweiler simply ripped his upper jaw free, slinging blood in a semi-circular pattern.

With accelerated power born of searing rage, Thorn again pressed his advantage at Maston's neck and chest.

The white-hot pain in his torn upper jaw expressed itself in even more intense shaking of his head, as he ripped at the underside of his rival.

It was a moment when the hot blood of his father pounded through his veins.

Other members of the Thicket Pack formed a circle, jumping toward the fighting dogs, and then bouncing back from the froth-filled jaws and ripping toenails that were sending saliva and dust into the air. All the spectating canids were lending their yelps and barks to the growls and snarls coming from Maston and Thorn. The violent battle was a fight to the death.

[67]

Thorn managed to get fully astraddle of Maston. Twice he used the sharp claws on his right rear foot to rip down across the tender tissue of the hound's waist. The second tearing stomp cut two deep grooves across the belly in front of Maston's left rear leg. Blood flooded from the wound, soaking, and further darkening Maston's auburn-colored hair.

Frantic and panicked by the growing realization of his injuries, Maston exploded to his feet, and began to run for the creek. Thorn gave chase, delivering a deep, muscle-tearing bite to Maston's lower right hip before breaking off his pursuit.

A few minutes later, Maston was curled up under a canopy of limbs and small, twisted tree trunks that had been deposited at the high water mark beside Shady River. Blood issued from his chest and stomach, before disappearing into the wet, sandy soil. The spot in which he'd chosen to hide became a hiding place for his bones.

Having led his Pack north for several months to explore new territory and re-think things following the death of two Pack members, Thorn was back, victorious in every sense of the word, and leading a group of ferals no less threatening than the one led by his father in years past.

Nine

Malya's Migration

In the middle of the twentieth century, the panthers that remained in the central part of Florida could be counted on one hand. The vast majority of the western mountain lion's close cousins had long since made their way to swamps at the southern end of the state.

Poaching, collisions with motor vehicles, overall encroachment by Obtruders, and resulting habitat degradation, along with predation on the young by the Florida alligator, conspired to kill off or drive out all but a very few of the magnificent cats.

Malya may well have been the last of her kind to leave the area north of today's Blue Spring State Park in Volusia County. She and her two cubs had been shot at twice in previous months. Each time it seemed the protracted run for safety took them further north – an odd circumstance when all others of her kind were heading south.

Even at 8-years-old, Malya remained an impressive animal. Her legs looked longer than the typical female. Her weight was well above average at just over 100 pounds. She approached 7-feet in length, and stood 32-inches tall at the shoulder.

Her coat was a soft rusty-buff, while her underbelly, chest, and muzzle appeared whiter than most Florida panthers. Her cubs' coloration was more fawn-like, much like their father.

The only noticeable blemishes to her otherwise striking appearance was the kink in her tail – likely the expression of a regressive gene due to the decades-old practice of inbreeding. The other was the milky-white color in her left eye, which had been damaged in a fight with a wild hog when Malya was 3-years-old. She retained only 10% of the vision on her left side.

Almost 40 miles north of their home territory, the felines continued with a just-keep-moving quality in their pace. When they could pick it up they did, and when they felt the need for increased caution, they dialed things back.

For extended periods the cubs would focus more on the mesmerizing sway at the tip of their mother's tail than on a panoramic view of the surroundings. As had been the case from day one of their trek, it was Malya's responsibility to remain watchful for highways and the always-confusing traffic. Second only to the rogue hunter's bullet, roadways provided the greatest threat to their wellbeing as they traveled.

Only two weeks into the journey, squalling tires and the blaring air horn of an 18-wheeler served to re-launch and re-energize the migration. Their movement was steady, and toward the North, always toward the North.

Typically, with Malya's kind, males were less reticent to cross paved roads than were females. There just seemed less caution in the male of the species. Even with her natural inclination toward caution, the near-miss with the flatbed wasn't the first nor would it be the last road-crossing in which Malya's tentativeness would nearly get her and the cubs killed.

>>><<<

As each narrow escape strengthened the urge to increase the pace toward a new, secluded home, Malya's feeling of being in control was beginning to weaken. Lack of self-confidence had never been a problem for the usually clear-headed and decisive cat.

She'd always been quick to engage in the challenge of caution-driven decision-making. But of late it was the overall task of dealing with the decision-making process that had begun to make Malya feel as though something just wasn't right.

It wasn't the tension of this-or-that at the heart of a decision that troubled Malya; it was the distinct feeling that the rationale behind a decision was becoming increasingly conflicted.

Clarity was being replaced with a growing sense of tentativeness – even disorientation.

In the months to come, her suspicions were to be confirmed. Something was indeed wrong, and the circumstance would only worsen.

>>><<<

About midday in the northern end of Duvall County near the Georgia-Florida state line, Malya and her cubs took refuge in tree tops that had been pushed into a 6-foot-high berm around the edge of a field at a county landfill.

The spot proved to be more roomy and comfortable than had first appeared, after the cats pulled small pine limbs and needles into a pile to soften hardened clods of dirt.

The landfill's brush and tree-trimming piles were a welcomed improvement over previous places the Panthers had slept: under the backend of a flatbed trailer in an open field, next to a rotting pile of firewood stacked alongside a rural community center building and beneath the wooden deck around an above-ground swimming pool.

For one of the few times on the trip, all three cats felt they could relax. The tightly-packed tree and brush trimmings provided excellent cover, and more importantly, that tension-relieving sense of security.

After settling in, Steed moved closer to his sister and spoke softly. "I could not have taken another day without something to eat. Catching the bird at the lake was good for us all. Thank you," said Steed as he lowered his head closer to his weakened sister's back. Steed and his mother were both aware the grueling travel seemed to be taking more of a toll on Tally than on either of them.

Looking in the opposite direction, Tally blinked twice, and managed a small, smile-like twitch in her upper lip. She loved and respected her brother. His encouragement and kind words were always appreciated.

Early that morning, all three predators had seen the Blue Heron at the same time. But it was Tally that got the closest, and sprung the trap. For three panthers, two of which were large and still-growing cubs, the 7-pound meal was meager. However, the plump water bird helped blunt the hunger pangs which were the cats' constant companion.

>>><<<

Following a zigzag pattern, the migrating Panthers were capable of covering as much as 13 to 15 miles per day. But the average was held under 10 by the need to pick their way around and through developed areas.

As with all large cats, there was that natural abundance of caution which served to slow their pace, especially in an unfamiliar, populated environment.

They were slowed by the ever-present possibility of barking dogs, highway traffic, and a growing weakness brought on by inadequate nourishment.

Three rabbits, a pair of squirrels, four chickens, the remains of three large pizzas, a three-foot alligator, and a medium-sized doe, killed by a car, made up the bulk of their intake since leaving the Daytona area.

They drug the recently-killed deer into the woods, and stayed close for almost three days eating the carcass.

The predators' nature was to be active at night, and rest during the day. That natural preference helped conceal their presence as they moved from field to field, wooded stretch to wooded stretch, and, at times, yard to yard. However, the trade-off for long periods of heightened caution was heightened tension and the resulting fatigue.

>>><<<

Just after sundown, when the three cats began to stir, the gnawing hunger was as strong as ever. Malya faced a simple reality; she and her cubs must hunt; they must hunt that evening; and they must hunt successfully.

Since leaving the east coast of Florida, they had not engaged in any serious hunting. With a single exception, each time they found something to eat it was purely good fortune. The exception was the alligator, which was stalked, cornered in the shallows and killed. The kill was a team effort.

At eleven months, Tally and Steed had been hunting with their mother for almost a year, beginning when they were just two months old.

[75]

That night, they would do their part in a classic hunt for prey large enough to stem the gradual loss of calories and energy they'd experienced for weeks.

And yet, even as their physical strength was down, their familial bond was up. The trials involved in the trip north had reinforced their sense of interdependency and mutuality.

This was partially evidenced by Malya taking time to lick and groom her cubs each time they awoke. It was something they enjoyed, and something their mother never failed to do – even with Steed at 75 and Tally just over 60-pounds.

Often between the slow strokes with her tongue, Malya would whisper things to her offspring. Several licks were drawn from Tally's nasal arch to the back of her head before Malya paused. Drawing close to her daughter's ear, she showed her usual economy with words as she whispered: "Tally, we will eat well tonight. I promise."

There was no response from her weakened daughter. Rather it was Steed that spoke softly, but with conviction.

"Tally, I'm going to join mother in this hunt and we will succeed. That's my promise to you. I will fill our stomachs!"

Malya raised her head, and looked over at her son. His eyes had always pleased her, with the roundness challenging but not overpowering their classic slant.

Steed looked back at his mother, his ears standing erect and fully-rounded. When Malya studied her son's face, what caught her eye as much as anything was the diamond-shaped mark running horizontally across the tip of his muzzle. It was a bright pink, as it stood in sharp contrast to the coal-black surroundings of his nose.

She was moved to say something simple, but very much from her heart.

"Your sister and I love you, Steed. We both appreciate and take comfort in your strength." She shifted her head and shoulders to give her son several licks across his cheek and neck – the moment of tenderness he hoped was coming.

Pushing herself up to a sitting position, Tally shook her head, and tamed the hair on her chest with several long licks of her own. Following a second head-clearing shake, she called for action.

"Let's find our meal!"

That's exactly what they would do later that night. But finding and taking the meat would bring danger. As the three neared the midpoint of their migration, the night's events would prove as threatening as any they'd faced since leaving their historical home.

For Malya, the night's hunt would bring back memories of previous confrontations and great loss.

Ten

Heading for Trouble

In his day, many words could have been used to describe the Sumac's top boar – aggressive, pugnacious, ill-tempered, tempestuous, violent, certainly a bully of the first order.

But there was no word more apropos than "unpredictable". One moment Wartek was rooting in the moist Sumac soil, and the next he was launching an unprovoked attack on a hog half his size.

He knew the lower Shady River Basin well, particularly the wettest areas. It was not unusual for his weekly rounds to take him from the upper end of Horney Head Creek to the southern-most tip of the swamp, as much as a mile below the Hunting Club.

Any creature with average intelligence was well-advised to use caution should they encounter Wartek on one of his swamp-wide patrols.

Unpredictable? Absolutely! But many found his knee-jerk aggressive behavior more easily understood than his random, predator-like manner. As impulsive as the beast could be, there were times when his actions looked carefully thought out, calculated, almost akin to those of a full time stalk-and-throttle predator, such as a wolf or a bobcat.

Wartek often looked as though he was hiding, stalking, planning in advance the ambush of a prey item. It was a strange dichotomy indeed – blustering about in the morning, and then carefully laying out the logistics of an ambush attack in the late afternoon.

When attempting to understand Wartek's ways, it's important to note that the Sumac's wild hogs were among the smartest of all large mammals. Wartek was smart enough to know exactly what he was doing. On the one hand, he did things to reinforce his tough-guy status for its territorial implications. On the other, he followed one of the most primal impulses of any large, intelligent carnivore – the impulse to hunt, kill, and eat. It's just that Wartek did what he did while seeming so completely self-aware.

>>><<<

When it came to Wartek's tormenting ways, there was a singular exclusion when it came to selecting a target for his belligerent actions – the 2-year-old boar, Ezy.

It was not known if Ezy was one of Wartek's countless progeny, nor was it known if that would have made any difference. It had never seemed to influence the way he'd dispensed hostility in the past. Many of his victims were certainly his own offspring, some only two or three years removed.

An adequate rationale for the unlikely alliance was at best, unclear. Perhaps it was nothing more than an elemental attachment Ezy developed when the huge boar spent time with his mother's sounder. Or perhaps, attracted to Wartek's strength, Ezy chose to follow him off into the forest, and Wartek simply chose not to object.

Whatever the reason, Ezy's presence did nothing to temper Wartek's unruly ways. To the contrary, the younger boar joined his 6-year-old companion in most of the older boar's mayhem.

One morning, Ezy's attention was captured by a tom flying from the ground to a nearby tree. Ezy started in the direction of the gobbler's perch, when he noticed the hen standing near a clutch of eggs at the base of a water oak tree.

Ezy, doubling his pace, sent the hen into the tree a few feet below the tom.

Shortly, the boars were eating the great birds' young.

As was typical, it was Wartek getting the lion's share. Five of the eggs had hatched, while another three of the chicks were struggling to emerge from the shell.

The hen had only the night before completed four weeks of incubation. Now she was sitting 20-feet above the scene as the nest was ravaged.

Free from the shell, struggling to get out into the morning light or still fully inside the large, creamy-tan egg, the clutchlings had no chance. On many occasions, both boars had raided nests filled with turkey eggs. It was a choice meal.

"Allow me my share!" snapped Ezy, as he tried to shoulder Wartek to the side. His best effort made little difference in the position Wartek assumed over the nest. The bully's thoughtlessness was rivaled only by his bad table manners.

"Be still, Ezy, and insure you don't anger me!" replied the dominant boar, as he continued to consume more than his share of the turkeys' clutch.

"Why must you always abuse the source of your good fortune, Wartek? Often I'm responsible for finding our best food, and just as often you show no regard for the rewards I'm due."

Wartek didn't offer an immediate answer, as he ground one of the final shells and its contents into a crunchy, runny mix, a portion of which dripped from each corner of his mouth.

Considering his response before it was made, Wartek smugly replied, "You travel with me under the protection and status I provide, and that's your reward, Ezy."

As always, the boar's response was flavored with more than a little arrogance.

The contents of three eggs Ezy managed to pull from under Wartek's nose, one golden-orange yoke that had not been fertilized, and a few other scraps were all Ezy could claim before turning to follow Wartek, who had summarily began to walk away.

Even with Ezy, the closest thing to a real companion the huge loner had ever known, the brute called all the shots in his detached way. Wartek finished eating and simply walked off. Ezy could come along or he could go in the opposite direction. It would make little difference to Wartek.

The 2-year-old did what he always chose to do: followed Wartek toward the northwestern boundary of Sumac Swamp with no further comment on Wartek's always-me-first eating habits.

The pair was heading for a place where Wartek's bellicose ways would put him in the greatest danger of his life. He would soon become topic-number-one within the ranks of the most threatening group of hunters in the Shady River Basin.

As Ezy followed Wartek toward the upper end of the Sumac, Dr. Murray Laws' day of tree analysis and documentation was getting underway near the northern end of the Sumac Swamp.

Had the wild boars known of the activity planned by the researchers or had the researchers been aware of Wartek's destination and the hog's aggressive temperament, perhaps the tragedy to come could have been avoided.

Eleven

Wartek Makes the List

By mid-summer of 1960, Dr. Laws' study of Musclewood and Shady River Basin trees was well underway. Five days a week he and his team started early and finished late, as they tackled the herculean task of documenting the overall health of the forest's woody plants.

Red maple, scarlet oak, laurel oak, bald cypress, live oak, palmetto cabbage, longleaf and loblolly pine, dogwoods, American holly, eastern white pine, cherry laurel, black gum, hickory, and other specimens, large and small, found their place in the growing data base.

Early that Friday morning, as he'd done many times before, Murray Laws waved the group of ecology students together at the back of a state-owned swamp buggy. There were still a sizable number of inspection sheets to be prepared.

"Good morning," said Dr. Laws, standing in the back of swamp vehicle #2.

"Let me extend a welcome to all of you, and express my appreciation for your help. As I'm sure you already know, the sheets you're holding are very important to this project. The data they hold will become the foundation upon which our analysis and recommendations are based."

"For the several first-timers we have with us today, let me just briefly comment on the items we look for when we work a tree. As you can see on the sheet layout, the notation headings are as follows:

<u>Tree Inspection Items</u>

1. <u>Status of New Leaves and Buds</u>
2. <u>Twig Growth</u>
3. <u>Mature Leaf Size vs. Standard</u>
4. <u>Unusual Trunk and/or Limb Deformity</u>
5. <u>Crown Dieback</u>
6. <u>Leaf Discoloration</u>
7. <u>Deformed Growth</u>
8. <u>Mushrooms and Conks on the Trunk</u>
9. <u>Dying in the Canopy or Limbs</u>
10. <u>Insect Activity of Any Type</u>

Dr. Laws offered comment on each item.

"Of course, don't be reluctant to use your camera. In this business, both today and down the road, a picture really is worth a thousand words. Also, don't hesitate to use your radio to call with any questions you may have. Should you encounter a classification issue or anything else deserving of more detailed evaluation, please call me or Mr. Harts, and one or both of us will come to you."

Murray Laws' top assistant on the project was Bernard "Bernie" Harts, a graduate student at the University of Georgia. Bernie was nearing the end of his work on a PhD. The students assisting Harts and Dr. Laws all came from the University of South Carolina or the University of Georgia. Each would be receiving academic credit for their field work in the Basin.

That morning, there were few questions following Murray Laws' comments, since most of the day's students had previously worked on the program.

>>><<<

As with the pending arrival of Wartek, the Laws group was unaware of additional eyes and ears attending the morning meeting. All were tuned in to the Obtruders that would be moving through the Musclewood Forest northwest of Horney Head Creek.

Members of the Sandy Knoll group had followed the tree-to-tree movements of the program's volunteers since the activity began. Enid's keep-your-eyes-open policy had become a mainstay in his strategy for serving the interests of the Carolina Pack.

[86]

Bren's father had come to believe the more he knew about what was going on in his section of the Basin, the more he was able to respond rather than react. Perhaps the wisest of the Sandy Knoll Pack, Enid understood the value of knowing what you should know.

The business of territorial awareness was something he seldom mentioned to other Pack members. But it was clearly something other protectors of the Sandy Knoll territory had picked up on. It was one of the fundamental, unspoken lessons strong leaders like Enid taught by example.

"They continue to move closer to our home," said Bren, who now at 9-months was joining his father more frequently on trips into the woods, both to observe and to hunt.

"That I can see, Bren," replied Enid.

"Unless they come much closer, I don't feel it needs to be at the center of our concern. But I do continue to question the purpose of these Obtruders' arrival. I have seen them only be involved with the trees. Our trees are where they show interest, not in the location of our den."

"Enid, I'm with Bren worrying about this Out World group moving so close to Sandy Knoll," said Chesman, who had been watching quietly from a few yards away.

"They may love our trees, but we know they have no love for us!" said Gwenfar's brother, once again sounding miffed by Enid's persistent inclination toward tolerance of Obtruder incursions. When irritated, most of Chesman's words came across as somewhat reckless and rushed.

"Chesman, if our response is to be effective, we must first know their intentions. To this point, I've seen nothing in their actions calling for us to threaten this group of Obtruders or encourage them to respond to us as enemies."

Once again, the logic of Enid's even-handed thinking left another male in the Sandy Knoll Pack searching for an agitation-inspired follow up.

Aware, but less focused than the Sandy Knoll canids, two members of the Thicket Pack had already come and gone before the last of Murray Laws' students divided up and headed toward their assigned research sectors. Not until only Murray and Bernie Harts remained with the swamp buggies in the makeshift base camp did Enid, Bren, and Chesman slip away.

Eleven pairs of students spread out to begin surveying the western side of West Horney Head Creek. A little further to the northwest Wartek and Ezy foraged in the soft soil on what would be a pivotal day for so many associated with the lower Shady River Basin.

Befuddling and unexpected terror was only minutes away.

>>><<<

Samantha Wyatt, a USC senior, was working about 20 feet from the west branch of Horney Head. The Florence, SC, native was in her third day with the Laws party. Her work had been right on the mark, and her enthusiastic involvement much appreciated by Laws and Bernie Harts.

A little before noon, Samantha was sitting back on her heels at the base of a black gum tree. It was probably her concentration on paperwork that caused her to miss Wartek's muted grunt. He'd been watching the co-ed for a while. His lowered head and unblinking eyes could only be called eerie.

Rather than fleeing at the Obtruder's approach, as any other boar would likely have done, Wartek chose to stand perfectly still. He was concealed in an area of small oaks, pines, and buttonbush. Slowing his breathing, and remaining motionless, he was able to hide in full view as Samantha, focused on the task at hand, moved to within mere yards of where he was standing.

As she stood and stepped back to take a picture of some non-typical growth on a Water Oak, her partner, Max Mullinax, radioed a question. With no more than a twitch, Wartek shifted his eyes from Samantha's face to the radio she'd removed from her belt.

[89]

"Sam, where'd you get to?"

Samantha keyed her Motorola. "I'm up here in front of you a ways," replied Samantha, as she began to gather up her materials.

"Okay, I'm headed your way. I want to get a drink of water," transmitted Max, as he started to jog in the direction he thought Samantha had gone. The perky redhead had left camp with the pair's only canteen.

It may have been the squelchy radio, Samantha's quick steps toward the next tree, or a combination of the two that set the beast in motion.

In two quick bounds, Wartek was into the grad student, slinging his head from side to side, and the coed with it. The hog alternated grunts and high-pressure squeals as he drove his front legs deeper into the ground, broadening his base and generating greater force.

The searing pain of slashes by bloodied tusks; Wartek's stomps into Samantha's mid-section with sharp, cloven hooves; and, perhaps the most bizarre element in the terrifying moments of the attack......the putrid smell of the hog's breath as the beast tried to focus on his victim's face, throat and upper chest.

It was the over-powering smell coming out of the hog's mouth that Samantha would later say

[90]

she remembered most about the horrifying moments.

The randomness of his movements spoke to the frenzied nature of his attack. There was no rhyme or reason, just an interest in doing as much damage as possible, as quickly as possible.

The giant boar didn't sound or look as though he was acting out of alarm, nor did he sound as though his territorial instincts were involved. What he sounded like was mean, very mean!

"Oh God!" cried Samantha as she tried to cover her face with her right arm, while hitting at her attacker with the clipboard she clutched in her hand. The attempts to protect herself only slowed Wartek once, when one of Samantha's blows sent the corner of her clipboard into the soft socket area under Wartek's left eye.

"Max! Max! He's killing me!" screamed Samantha as Wartek used his powerful head and neck to roll the small woman over and over at the base of the tree she'd just surveyed. Samantha was right. His intention was to kill her!

"Samantha! Samantha, I'm coming!" yelled Mullinax, using his forearms to knock away head-high branches as he raced in the direction of his partner's cries.

The scene grew clearer as Max neared the water's edge. Now able to see, as well as hear the boar's rage, the muscular 22-year-old never slowed. He ran directly toward the hog as he shouted into his radio for help.

Ignoring the medium-sized knife on his belt, the former University of Georgia football player slowed only long enough to scoop up a stick from the ground.

Wartek, momentarily taken aback by Mullinax's arrival on the scene, broke to his right away from Samantha. His retreat was quick, but not quick enough to keep Mullinax from breaking the sizable limb across the exaggerated, boney ridge running almost the entire length of Wartek's back.

He took the opportunity to retrieve the radio, which had fallen to the ground in the melee. Again he called for the help that was already headed in their direction.

That's when Wartek did the unthinkable. He returned to continue his assault on Samantha.

Mullinax couldn't believe his eyes as the enraged animal raced back in their direction, striking Samantha in the ribcage on her left side.

Max was able to use the largest and hardest remaining piece of the limb to land a vicious blow on the left side of Wartek's head – a blow that sent the attacker into the woods to stay.

>>><<<

Samantha Wyatt was admitted to the hospital with punctures, cuts, abrasions, and broken ribs. She was there for several trying and painful weeks. All involved, including Samantha, knew she was fortunate to be alive.

Had Max not seen him return for a second time to continue his attack, showing what was very much an atypical level of aggression, the only headache Wartek may have faced was the one associated with the second blow, resulting in a ruptured lower gum and painful gash where a tusk was almost pinched through the cheek between the jaw and Max Mullinax's makeshift club.

However, when members of the Shady River Hunting Club heard of the extended attack by the jumbo-sized, rust-colored boar, he was promptly added to their "special projects list" – a headache Wartek couldn't have anticipated when he jumped ugly with the Carolina co-ed.

It was a list no Basin animal would ever want to make. In the past, targets included several predators whose aggression had been directed toward livestock or household pets.

A bobcat with a taste for beagles and other small hunting dogs; an obviously psychotic buck that enjoyed nothing more than randomly goring other deer; and an assortment of feral dogs had fallen victim to the coordinated hunting efforts of the club's membership.

Club President, Clinton Dunlap, summarized things well. "We'll avenge that young lady's injuries. It's just a question of where and how soon. That bad boy's days are numbered."

Twelve

Food Fight

Not until Malya awoke and worked her way to the outside did she know there had been a heavy shower. The pile of treetops was so tightly packed together, little water reached the spot where she'd slept.

The dry interior of the treetop pile had enticed her, Steed, and Tally to sleep longer than usual. The rest helped, but the most urgent need was still finding something substantial to eat.

Steed followed close behind his mother, exiting the pine tops just to her left hip. In his haste, he bumped one of the larger limbs, releasing the water it held onto the top of his mother's head.

As the water showered down, Malya said nothing. She simply stopped, slowly turned her head to the left, and flashed that widened, white, and yellow eyeball.

The scar which ran across the top lid, stretching the corner an inch downward toward her cheek, helped her redefine the notion of giving someone "the evil eye". It wasn't the first time Steed succeeded in earning that special look.

Watching as her son lowered his head, Malya said only, "Stop, and wait until I step outside." It was more than adequate to communicate the flash of irritation with her son's insolence.

Tally waited until the passageway was clear to join her mother and brother outside the brush pile. All three cats stood and surveyed the perimeter of a 3-acre field, surrounded by mounds of residential brush trimmings and cut trees. Once county residents emptied their pickups and contractors their dump trucks, landfill workers bulldozed the limbs and brush up against a growing pile of woody debris around the field's perimeter.

In darkness, deepened by the overcast sky, Malya led the cubs directly across the open field. She was headed for a dirt road which led out of the encircling brush piles, and skirted another field where metal refuse containers were staged. Their contents were being readied for compaction in a nearby building.

Walking softly behind their mother, Tally turned to Steed with a question.

"What do you think she's considering brother – a deer or perhaps, if we can find one, a thick-skinned hog?"

"I don't know which way her thoughts are going tonight. She's said nothing, and she's indicated no choice to me. You know how she's gotten in recent months. She has little to say about most things anymore. And, when it's said, I'm often not sure what she means."

Steed continued to think about Tally's question over the next few steps behind their mother.

"I think it more likely to be a deer than a strong hog. Hogs fight hard, and the effort required to take one would be more exhausting than what we would likely face with a deer."

"Steed, I hope you know I will do my part at the kill, regardless of what prey her skills provide. I've come to dread the hunger and its growing power over me more than any struggle with strong prey," said Tally, as the two cubs picked up the pace to catch up with Malya.

Before the night was over, determination and full commitment to the task at hand would prove more to the point than either knew.

>>><<<

The third staging area of the electric-blue rollaway dumpsters was the last the cats would pass before coming to the gate in a high, chain-link fence.

Prior to reaching the dumpster with "18" stenciled on the side, they walked by several frontend loaders, an assortment of pickup trucks, a track hoe, a small gate-attendant building, and a flatbed trailer loaded with scrap metal. Looking at the assortment of jumbo-sized metal equipment, there was no doubt the cats were deep within a place occupied and probably patrolled by Obtruders.

Number 18 was sitting third in line from the fence, perpendicular to the paved road that passed under the front gate to intersect with the county road just outside. The spot where the bright blue rollaway container sat was the place where the evening's real action began.

A half-grown doe bolted from between #18 and an older rollaway dumpster sitting to its left. Once on the pavement, she turned to the right in front of the three cats. The deer's hooves clicked and rattled on the blacktop, as she drove forward looking for quick acceleration.

In contrast, all three cats came to speed on pads that made no sound.

For Malya and the cubs, a flash of alarm had instantly given way to the primal instinct in all felines. Each exploded forward, quickly matching the speed of the deer.

Pursued by an animal able to leap 45-feet, jump 15-feet high, and reach speeds of 45 miles per hour, the deer's fate was sealed if she continued to run in a straight line.

Steed was close behind his mother, when he swung out to Malya's left in order to gain more perspective on their target.

Twenty feet ahead, both Panthers saw the flash for which the whitetail is named. The deer made its second right turn to sprint along the fence. She was heading to a place at the back of the enclosure where a fallen tree had recently lowered the fence from 7 to just over 3-feet high.

That's where she'd entered the fenced-in area, and it was where she intended to exit.

Steed's sister hadn't joined him in running behind their mother. Rather she had taken a 45-degree angle by the rear corner of the dumpster. She was headed for a point 60-yards down the fence line in hopes of heading off the quarry.

Seeing Tally angling in from the right, the terrified doe gathered up the additional speed that comes only from desperation and pulsing panic. The doe managed to race beyond the point of Tally's intended attack. Tally fell in line, only a few yards behind the deer, missing with the swipe of a paw intended for the doe's right rear leg.

With Tally in head-long pursuit, and her mother and brother only a few yards behind, the deer dug even deeper, and managed to reach the low spot in the fence ahead of her pursuers. With no wasted motion, her leap put several feet between herself and the barbed wire strung along the top of the downed fence.

Looking much like participants in some synchronized midnight steeplechase, the three cats flew in formation over the galvanized metal fence. It looked as though a kill was imminent.

In the next instant, Malya brought the effort to an abrupt halt. She didn't see the five wooden pallets stacked up only a few feet from where she'd landed. The old wood had blackened, and her left eye was more troublesome at night.

The collision was sudden and frightening as the rotting planks seemed to explode with the 100-pound cat's impact. For the most part, Malya tumbled over the top of the pallets before skidding to a stop in the wet grass.

Had things been different; if her vision had been what it was before the boar attack 5 years earlier; if the night had not been so dark under the overcast skies, and if the chase hadn't been super-heated by the powerful billows of hunger, Malya would have easily and gracefully cleared the pile of decaying pallets.

Both cubs bounced to a stop. Their mother soon realized she was more startled than injured, although there were two superficial, but nasty-looking abrasions – one on her chest, and the other almost the length of her right upper lip. But, by far, her greatest concern was the loss of the deer.

"Mother, are you alright?" asked Tally.

"I'm alright, and I'm sorry that my mistake let the deer escape."

Steed had said nothing; he was unaccustomed to seeing his mother miss her prey, particularly in such an embarrassing and disarming way. Malya was strong and proud; her misses most often came when prey reached deep water, a well-constructed den or the covering-protection of an Obtruder's building.

>>><<<

As Tally moved to Malya and began to nuzzle the neck of her still-dazed mother, the first sounds came through the trees. They were sounds of an attack – sounds of a violent encounter, snarls, growls, and the unmistakable moment of predation.

Malya had heard the hoarse, guttural sounds before. They were chilling sounds from her youth – haunting sounds with great staying power.

After pausing to listen and think, it was Malya's choice to lead the cubs further into the woods. She moved in the direction taken by the deer. Her gait was guarded, and her scanning of the trees ahead both cautious and deliberate.

The unmistakable sounds of a kill had gone silent, but the Panthers were now close enough to see the scene for themselves. It was what Malya knew they would see.

The fleeing, panic-stricken doe had run into a small clearing surrounded by thick brush. It was the occasional home of a sizable female black bear. Unfortunately for the doe, that night the sow was eating berries just off the edge of the clearing.

Before she broke into the opening, the bear had been able to hear, and smell the doe coming. After the cats broke off the chase, the deer had slowed, but her momentum was still in play.

Standing thirty yards away, it looked to Malya and the cubs as though the bear had simply exploded from the undergrowth, and gone for the exhausted animal's vitals. In all likelihood, death came in the sow's jaws as quickly as could be expected.

"Mother, the deer ran right into the bear's grasp," said Steed, as he tried to take in every detail of the scene before him.

"The deer did better with us than it did with the bear. We know that, Steed," observed Malya, as she tried to ignore the distraction of the stinging, blood-red scrape along her upper lip.

Even to an experienced animal like Malya, a forest dweller that had seen many things, watching a black bear kill and eat a nearly-grown whitetail was unusual.

The sow may have been just as pleased had she stumbled upon a pile of acorns. But a nearly-defenseless, already-weakened deer, one that looked and smelled like pure opportunity, was irresistible stimulation that ignited her deepest predatory instinct.

The Panther's watched as the bear bit into the doe, trying to open the chest cavity in order to expose the heart and other nutritious organs.

Watching the scene grow bloodier and more compelling, the cats felt increased agitation and anger that always comes with feeling snookered.

In times past, other predators had tried to steal their kill. Twice the thief was a marauding black bear, and both times the bear was successful.

If Malya and her cubs' best efforts could make a difference, that night it would be the cats that claimed the prize.

With sharply focused eyes, head and neck lowered, Tally was first to start the approach. Appearing as though she was on tiptoes, small, measured, super-silent steps grew into a muscular sprint toward the bear. To the feisty female's benefit, the bear was facing in the opposite direction as Tally began her assault.

Flanked by Malya on the left, and Steed on the right, Tally accomplished the initial objective. The bear was taken completely by surprise and thoroughly rattled as the cats suddenly materialized in the clearing.

Spinning to her right, lowering her head and backing away from the doe, the sow instinctively dropped her hind-quarters, and prepared to take on the Panthers.

With Tally facing the bear head on, Malya, just off the bear's right shoulder, and Steed positioned to the sow's left, the stage was set.

All three Panthers knew full well the fight was nothing to be taken lightly. Even with the numbers standing at three-to-one in the cats' favor, the likelihood of successfully inflicting life-threatening injury favored the bear. The fully-grown sow was the real deal.

She had a tough hide; a heavy layer of fat; muscular shoulder plates; claws longer than those of the Panthers; jaws that could easily splinter bone; surprisingly quick reflexes; and muscle power in a single arm capable of turning over rocks exceeding her own weight. There was simply no other animal native to the Basin that possessed both the defensive and offensive package of weapons found in a full-grown black bear.

With terrifying speed and explosive power, the sow was more than capable of ripping a panther to pieces in a matter of seconds.

Malya's eyes darted between her young and the bear. She could only hope Steed and Tally understood the full extent of the threat.

As she took her position and prepared to face the strapping predator, Malya's mind also flashed back to that terrible day she'd witnessed a bear attack taken to its brutal conclusion. It was etched deeply in her memory, and with good reason.

At just under a year old, Steed and Tally's mother had watched as two Florida panthers joined forces in facing a large boar that was protecting it kill. The fight was on in an instant, becoming extremely fierce, very bloody, and lasting over 15 minutes.

[105]

In the end, the cats, a female and young male, were overpowered and partially dismembered by the enraged bear. Known only to Malya those many years earlier, the female that fell to the boar's crushing jaws was her mother.

Steed flew into the sow's left side, causing her to wheel in his direction. With the bear's head turned, Malya sank her teeth into its right shoulder, furiously shaking her entire body, before retreating to a safer distance.

A battle tactic featuring first-you-then-me had been used before by Malya and her cubs, but never on a creature more threatening than the large, fully-outraged bear.

The danger would come at the end of the charge, where the slightest miscalculation in beginning the retreat could prove lethal. Malya understood the single thing that made bears such threatening adversaries. It was a quality belied by their size. She could only hope her young sensed the contradiction in the sow's great bulk and it *unanticipated speed*.

Knowing to avoid jaws capable of breaking her neck, Tally took the opportunity to attack the sow's vulnerable left side. The response she received erased any doubt Tally may have had as to the lightening quick responses of her adversary.

The bear jerked its head back to the left with such power it knocked Tally to the ground, sending her rolling several yards across the scuffed floor of the clearing.

Incapable of roaring, all three cats were growling and snarling, doing everything possible to convince the bear of their commitment to the task at hand.

The series of well-coordinated strike-and-retreat maneuvers were effective in ultimately sending the bear scrambling for cover. The painful nips to her shoulders, sides, and rump became more than she could stand.

Only Steed gave chase, reveling in the family's moment of triumph in routing one of the deep woods' fiercest carnivores. "We did it," announced his sister, proudly proclaiming the obvious, as Steed trotted back from the brief pursuit.

"Yes we did, sister. The deer is ours."

As always, the quiet, serious-minded Malya was tending to business. She had already surveyed the deer's remains, and begun dragging it toward cover. There was plenty of meat still on the bones. Both the successful efforts at vanquishing the bear, and the still-warm meat were hugely satisfying. Their hunger was tempered and the family's confidence buoyed.

After eating for several minutes, Tally turned to her brother with a thought in the form of a question. "Steed, what was it you said about taking a hog being more difficult than taking a deer?"

For the next two days, the road-weary cats rested and ate well.

Thirteen

Life's Rhythms in the Summer of '60

The summer of 1960 was a scorcher! With daytime temperatures routinely climbing above 100 degrees, and little relief coming with nightfall, animals of the Basin throttled back their activities in favor of slowing down and finding ways to blunt the day's heat.

Daily hunts, weekly scouting of territorial perimeters, periodic settling of disputes within the social unit, and the annual rites of birth and death were maintained, but at a noticeably slower pace. The particularly oppressive heat that year made the deep woods animals more lethargic and less venturesome.

Creatures of the swamp stayed near or in the water, while those living in dens sought relief underground or among the rocks.

For animals along Shady River mid-summer was always the slowest time of the year; but in 1960 the oppressive heat was particularly stifling.

>>><<<

Thorn and the Thicket Pack were well-settled in their Rock Cave den. They hadn't proven to be the malevolent presence Enid, Ingrum, and other deep forest dwellers had feared.

That's not to say they hadn't been a threat to others in the Basin. The Thicket Pack was particularly problematic for Norvel and Wilma Ross.

Thorn and other males found two places in the Ross fence line where wild hogs frequently tore down wire to gain entry into the pasture. Once in, the hogs liked to eat the scatterings of grain around the Holstein's feed troughs. Another treat was cooling off with a wallow in the wet, muddy, feces-ladened mud found in several places on the farm.

Hunting in the cooler evening hours, the Thicket Pack managed to take two calves and one small Holstein heifer. The night the heifer was killed Norvel and Wilma were out of town, and the local man they'd hired to feed the cattle did little else. Each calf was eaten in a single feeding session, while Thorn led the Pack back three days in a row to feed on the cow.

In 1960, there was one significant interruption of the Thicket Pack's summer routine – the loss of a valued member.

Wiston was investigating a burrow in a patch of palmetto when he surprised an enormous eastern diamondback. The thick-bodied struck instantly from just inside the shallow weasel den, hitting the shepherd mix breed in the right jaw.

He reacted almost as quickly, jerking his head back and pulling the entire six-foot snake out onto the ground, still writing and tugging at Wiston's jaw. .

The broad-headed viper wedged a fang in the feral's jawbone as both tried to withdrawn at the same instant.

It was an odd thing to see – the lightning-fast snake's strike stopped at the point of contact, like a boxer's quick jab failing to return from an opponent's chin.

Shaking himself free from the serpent, Wiston retreated. But his fate was sealed.

He'd been bitten by the largest venomous snake in North America. The muscular poison gland had pressurized the snake's fangs with enough blood-destroying venom to kill a large dog several times over. Wiston suffered terribly, and died within the hour.

The aging, well-established diamondback moved away beneath its favorite saw palmetto plants, having again taken the life of an unsuspecting predator of the deep woods.

[111]

At The Wash, Ingrum and his family were following their well-established, mid-summer routines. The opportunistic hunters kept busy pursuing rodents, rabbits, birds, and other small vertebrates. Especially in the dead of summer, invertebrates such as insects, and even worms were on the menu.

Ingrum and his vixen were a bit out of the ordinary, in that they enjoyed fruits and even some vegetables available in nearby gardens. From time to time, they also went to the water, eating fish and frogs. To describe Ingrum's, Pixlee's, and the kits' menu as varied is quite an understatement. They ate it all, from crawfish to corn.

Of course, the foxes never overlooked treats to be found in Obtruder garbage cans. Food found there came with little effort, and no exhausting daytime hunt.

There was one troubling development which Ingrum and his family faced in the steamy summer of '60. A pair of coyotes made their way from northeast Louisiana to the lower end of Shady River Basin. The male, Lodren, and his mate, Cunea, were living in an earthen den in the eastern part of the Lower Musclewood. The den location put the transplants well within Ingrum's home territory.

He'd first encountered them while eating remains where the Thicket Pack killed the cow on the Ross Dairy Farm. The medium-sized canids were both aggressive in claiming a share, particularly the female. When Ingrum crossed paths with those two, he knew good judgment mandated they be given a wide berth. Failure to do so could cost him his life.

Ingrum had long known things could get dicey fast when food or territory was at issue. Each coyote outweighed him by 15 to 20 pounds. Should they join forces, Ingrum would stand no chance.

>>><<<

As for the Sandy Knoll Pack, Enid and other members spent much of the summertime in or near Sumac Swamp. They were comfortable with the idea of being in the wet areas. The Carolina Dogs naturally took to water, as evidenced by their webbed front toes. Often they would choose to walk in the rivers or streams rather than stay in the edge of the woods along the banks.

At about seven months, with no new pups on the scene, and none on the way, Bren, Banner, Modred and Castle were the youngest members of the Pack. They were learning quickly, and the swampier areas of the Sumac offered an instructive divergence from the dry, elevated Knoll.

Enid and Bree allowed the four a good deal of freedom, but were always mindful of the need to correct or help when their young stumbled.

At, or just over a year old, Seph and Bedwyr's pups, along with the pups of Corvin and

Gaius were active, contributing members of the Pack. In addition, the four were playing a large part in exposing Enid and Bree's young to life on the hammocks, in the pine forests, and along the waterways of the lower Shady River.

One change did take place that summer which altered life for the Sandy Knoll dogs. The former pariah, Captain, disappeared about dawn one morning in early July. He was there at midnight, and the next morning he was nowhere to be found.

Having spent a good portion of his life among Obtruders in the Out World, the degree of socialization he brought along when finally accepted by Enid and the other Carolina Dogs, never quite permitted seamless integration into the Pack.

Enid didn't like loose ends, and Captain's disappearance bothered the group's dominant male.

"Enid, what do you think happened to Captain?" asked Bree, as she and her mate sat at the edge of a river feeder stream, watching the pups play in the edge of the water.

"I have no answer to that Bree. He never seemed to completely accept our ways, and I believe Wartek's tusk pierced more than his shoulder. I think it pierced his spirit. After Wartek's attack, he entered the woods with less conviction, less confidence. I believe his thoughts often returned to the Out World, and the peaceful task of lying at the Obtruders' feet, waiting for the next handout."

"His legs may have taken him back to the place his thoughts never fully left."

The wise and experienced leader's reasonings were more often right than wrong. But on that occasion, the analysis he offered contained little truth.

Just after dawn on the morning he disappeared, Captain chased a rabbit along a particularly deep muskeg. Running at the edge of the watery bed of rotting vegetation, along a path known to the rabbit as much by feel as by sight, the slate-gray buck turned sharply to the right, heading across the bog.

Captain followed at full speed – running and leaping beyond the point of no return.

It took the deadly suction just over 30 minutes to gain enough advantage from Captain's struggles to seal off the nostrils of the weakened feral.

Sitting half way up his favorite tree, Aster rotated then lowered his head, watching the last bubbles reach the surface. It was something the great horned owl had seen many times – one of the swamp's most deceptive bogs claiming a victim. Aster looked straight ahead, and kept his words as only thoughts....*another hunter finds no prey, only the worst the Sumac has to offer.*

Unable to move his eyes in their sockets, he lowered his head for one final look before pumping his great wings. He often soared high on the hottest days, where it seemed the air was cooler and more pleasant against his face.

>>><<<

Of course, the animals weren't alone dealing with the summer heat. So were their farming neighbors.

As usual, Raford "No-Toes" Thompson spent a great deal of time putting in, and tending his super-sized garden. Forced to work at a slower pace in the high temperatures, No-Toes was finally rewarded following his regimen of extra watering. His garden plot yielded beautiful vegetables.

Raford ate his share, and gave away a good portion to neighbors, even though they all had gardens of their own. The simple fact was no one in the area rivaled the almost one-acre effort for which No-Toes was renowned.

When it came to gardening, the time Raford spent tending plants was almost equaled by the time he devoted to keeping away animals with a taste for homegrown produce. The deer were a real challenge, with their seemingly boundless taste for sun-ripened tomatoes and crisp sweet corn.

No-Toes also spent time at the farmer's market where he rented a booth to sell his produce. Throw in the nights angling for catfish on the river, and No-Toes' summertime weeks were all but spoken for.

>>><<<

Taking steps to try and keep their pregnant Anglo-Nubian goats from overheating always consumed a large portion of Clinton and Peggy Dunlap's summer.

Back in '57, a bad year for flies, and a heavier-than-usual pinkeye outbreak, prompted the Dunlaps to initiate a fall kidding program. There was no scientific evidence of a direct connection between hot-weather flies and Pinkeye, but try and convince Clinton Dunlap of that.

In addition to the infectious fly issue, Clinton felt as though the scent of afterbirth was more detectible drifting on light summer breezes than on heavier, typically wetter winter air. Again, there was scant scientific verification, but with hungry predators watching from the woods and 80 nannies averaging two kids each per year, you play every angle.

The Dunlap goats were raised for milk. The Nubians weren't known for huge milk production, but their milk was higher in milkfat content than most, and highly in demand among folks who valued goat's milk.

The math was easy – plenty of goats meant plenty of chores. Including the year's newborns, the Dunlaps tended almost 200 animals over the course of a year, processing sizable production in milk, cheese, and some meat products.

When Clinton and Peggy started the project they'd long postponed, they did so in one of the hottest summers in decades. They set out to string new fencing around the three main pastures before the fall kids began to arrive.

It was the Thicket Pack's recent raids on the livestock which proved the final straw. Hotter-than-usual weather really couldn't be allowed to stand in the way.

"Murdock, look at this along here," shouted Clinton as he pointed down a 30-foot stretch of wire on the back side of the largest pasture.

Parker Murdock, who was helping Clinton run the new lines, shook his head as he surveyed the twisted wire crisscrossing pole-to-pole, two of which were completely down.

"With the hogs doing this kind of damage, it's a wonder we have a single head left in the pasture," added Clinton.

As fate would have it, the next morning Clinton and Parker found the scant remains of a young nanny that had been completely devoured, including bones. With only a few canine footprints around, it was clear from the chopped up ground and hoofed prints that hogs had done the deed.

"Boss, you reckon they ate her alive or ya think she was dead when they got to her?"

"God, I don't know, Parker. Guess they'd a killed her as soon as not," replied Norvel, standing over the few remaining splinters of bone and strips of hide with black and white hair still attached.

The first discovery of a goat fully-consumed by wild hogs provided further motivation for Clinton Dunlap to finish the fence, which at the very least would take the remainder of the sweltering summer days.

>>><<<

It was Ken and Ronda Moon that took first place in the deal-with-the-heat sweepstakes of 1960. The couple spent the entire summer on the coast of Maine. They had saved for years to take that one great extended vacation, and the steamy summer that year seemed just the right time to head north toward Ronda's childhood home. Ken, a 26-year employee with Carolina Southern Railway had retired the previous December.

>>><<<

With the attack on Samantha Wyatt overshadowing most everything, Murray and Ellen Laws' summer was difficult. Following three weeks in the hospital, which included plastic surgery on her right cheek, Samantha's family hired an attorney.

The State of South Carolina, the University, the State Forestry Commission and Dr. Murray Laws were all facing a potential lawsuit.

However, the state's attorneys felt confident things could be resolved without going to court. The matter did bring a temporary halt to Murray's research. Both USC and UGA stopped providing research assistants.

Murray was able to hire a few graduates, but the overall project was crippled.

There was something else stopped by Wartek's attack: Rory Laws' excursions into the forest. His mother wouldn't hear of him heading off into the woods, not with that kind of danger.

Even the elevated hunting stand his father bought for Rory to use in observing wildlife was declared off limits. Hopefully, time would help Ellen feel differently. But in the summer following the attack, even Murray joined his wife in insisting the kids stay near the house.

With what the fall and winter were to bring, the Laws' directives would prove more than justified.

Fourteen

Hunters, Hunger and Other Close Calls

Over the second half of their journey, finding secure places to hide, meeting the constant challenge of hunger, and dealing with the brutal heat took a real toll on Malya, Steed and Tally.

The relentless tension brought on by being out of their environment day after day had exhausted the three cats. Harrowing experiences came almost daily, each seeming more stressful than the one before.

On one occasion, just before dark, they crossed a fairway at a small private golf course. Seeing three large cats traveling together, two part-time groundskeepers hurried to spread the word about a "pack of mountain lions" roaming Glynn County. In the northern outskirts of Brunswick, armed locals were gearing up to hunt the Panthers down.

The following morning, acting more like raucous vigilantes than hunters, the group chased the cats with the help of dogs. Twice Malya, Tally and Steed were within rifle range. The first time no shot was taken, but the second time Malya and the cubs were flushed, the bullet kicked up dirt within feet of Steed.

There was little rest the next two days as the Panthers increased their pace, hoping to put distance between themselves, the baying hounds, and the hunters' rifles.

Two weeks back, west of Savannah, a bad automobile accident had put Malya and the cubs in a drainage culvert for more than three hours. The shouting, clanging, and clatter above their heads were nerve-wracking. The highway culvert experience only served to deepen the family's mental exhaustion and disorientation.

>>><<<

There was another trying experience which came near Bluffton, S.C., when two large dogs attacked Tally. Lagging behind her mother and brother at the time, she was taken by surprise as the dogs suddenly charged out of the woods to her left.

Individually, they wouldn't have struck the young Panther as all that threatening. However, together they looked to be more than a handful.

Good judgment and natural feline impulses argued for a quick escape up a tree, rather than taking on two snarling, muscled-up thugs. But Tally quickly saw the dogs were between her and the safety offered by a lone pine. Her quick judgment dictated she pass on a charge between the canines toward the tree.

All the 60-pound female could do was face the threat. Bearing her teeth, unsheathing and extending her claws, while lowering her head and broadening the base between her front legs, she prepared to do just that.

As Malya's daughter assumed the classic defensive position, she hoped her throaty snarls and lightning-quick sweeps of her paws would serve to discourage the dogs' charge.

If her bring-it-on posturing wasn't enough to give the dogs pause, one look at the narrowed vertical pupils resting just below the drawn-down eyelids might well suffice, at least until her mother or brother could turn back to help.

The dogs only thought Tally was something else. Malya was about to redefine the term, "bad news"

She barely slowed before exploding into the left shoulder of the cream-colored American pit bull. He didn't even have time to turn and face the cat. Had he been able to do so, it likely would have done little good.

The stocky canine was knocked onto its right side where Malya pressed the attack.

Tally's screams and snarls had succeeded in befuddling the canids. Any real confidence they may have had, based on the advantage of surprise, melted away in the heat of the cats' immediate, savage and combined response.

What Tally hadn't realized was that the two dogs were really no more than neighborhood bullies. The housecats they routinely chased into the trees and the young, nearby boxer they continually threatened were their usual victims.

That day, just inside the Bluffton, SC, city limits the two were not engaging some local stray they caught darting back and forth across the twosome's territorial boundary.

The Panthers' reaction was faster and more savage than anything the two had ever seen. For the impetuous attack, one would pay with his life.

Before the muscular dog could mount a defense, Malya sank her claws into its soft underside, while forcing her canines into the upper left side of its neck

As had happened so many times in the past, the slightly curved, 3-inch teeth found their mark.

Two twists of her head, and the dog's neck was broken. Even in her weakened condition, Malya exerted more than 300-pounds of bone-crushing power in dispatching the pit bull mixed breed – a powerful animal in its own right.

After briefly engaging Malya, the other dog made good its escape, with two 4-inch, parallel gashes in it left side.

Uncertain of just what to do, Steed and Tally stood near the dead dog, waiting for Malya to signal her intent.

With a note of hesitation, Steed turned to his mother. "What do we do now, mother?"

As often happened in recent weeks, Malya didn't answer. She simply pulled the dead pit bull to nearby brush, where she encouraged the hungry cubs to eat. Over the next three hours, Malya, Steed, and Tally filled their stomachs with the

[125]

muscular dog – an uncommon, but opportune meal.

>>><<<

For the past two weeks, the cats had passed through or skirted places that reminded them of home. But somehow Malya wanted to keep moving. Something told her they hadn't come to the place they were seeking.

That would change in less than two weeks, when the family moved beyond the mouth of the Savannah River, and arrived at the lower end of the much smaller Shady River Basin – a short distance from the southern tip of Sumac Swamp.

Fifteen

As Pertains to Wild Hogs

The Shady River Hunting Club always held its pre-fall meeting on the third Saturday in August. In 1960, the meal featured something different from traditional spreads like barbeque, grilled steaks or wildlife dishes such as venison, bear or elk.

Thirty-eight members and their spouses were treated to Lake Charles native Larry Landry's specialty – an authentic Louisiana boil.

Most folks came early to watch Larry fire up the 50-gallon cooker, and provide commentary as each colorful ingredient was dropped into the soft-boiling water.

"Okay, folks, let's begin with some yellow onions, unpeeled if you please," said Landry as he started his running narrative.

The remaining ingredients and several fun comments on each added to the evening. In addition to the large yellow onions, the poster-sized

"Boil Recipe" sitting on a tripod at the end of the table included:

- Crisp Celery Stalks
- Snappy-Fresh Garlic Cloves
- Bay Leaves
- A Cup of Sea Salt
- A Pound of Bright Red Cayenne Pepper
- Black Peppercorns
- 3 lbs of Red-Skin Potatoes (Unpeeled)
- 2 Dozen Live Blue Crabs (Yum, Yum, Eat-em-up)
- 12 Ears of Corn
- 6 lbs of Large Shrimp (Heads On Please) and
- Larry's Very Special and Very Secret Boil Spice Mix

There was no danger of anyone jotting down the recipe and stealing Larry's low-country thunder – not without the ingredients and proportions in the final item on the list.

>>><<<

After dinner, Clinton Dunlap called things to order, thanked Larry and his wife for the superb meal, and recognized a couple of special guests: Dr. Murray Laws and Frank Dooley. Dooley was with the South Carolina Wildlife and Marine Resources Department.

There were words of appreciation for all who helped with improvements recently made to the bath and shower rooms, as well as the fresh coat of paint applied to most of the 50-year-old building.

Several other items on the after-dinner agenda were brought before the group.

In addition to hunting in the Basin, the Club held hunting rights on two other properties. One was a tract of land north of Valdosta, GA, where the bird and deer hunting was excellent. The other was in southeastern Wyoming where members went for antelope and mule deer. Plans for hunts at each were outlined, followed by brief discussion.

>>><<<

As topics moved closer home, there was clearly interest in the "special projects list" and its newest addition.

The members' preferred game was far and away the whitetail deer. Hogs were hunted, but nothing like the whitetails. In the fifties, hunters in the Basin had begun to think in an organized way about hunting hogs, even though more traditional furred and feathered game held sway.

Conversely, hogs were beginning to think about hunters – as something to be avoided. The smart, resourceful animals were becoming more cautious and adaptive with every crack of the rifle.

Prior to the meeting, nothing had been done to follow up on the group's commitment to do away with the boar that attacked Samantha Wyatt. Now the time had come, and a few days before the dinner meeting a hunt had been put on the calendar.

Coming out of the hottest weather, things were beginning to change around the hunting lodge. Discussions turned toward the cooler temperatures of fall and the upcoming pre-rut and primary rut windows among the whitetails. All the area's wildlife was beginning to move. Wild hog sightings were on the increase, clearly indicating a growing willingness among the hogs to leave their cool, muddy hideouts. There was also the group's renewed interest in the Samantha Wyatt situation. Interest at the Club in ridding the Basin of a particularly dangerous animal was reenergized.

The evening was planned as an opportunity for club members to take a closer look at one of the Basin's dominant, but lesser understood animals.

>>><<<

Murray Laws spoke briefly, providing an update on the situation with Samantha, and its implications for his research project. He also made a few comments on wild hogs' impact on forest plant life – particularly trees.

"The harm they cause can be very subtle – most of it being done in the wetlands. Their rooting can accelerate the decomposition of leaf litter, and thereby hasten the loss of nutrients in the soil. That in turn stunts seeding growth, and ultimately the very young plants' survival. Longleaf pine seedlings seem to be particularly susceptible to wild pigs."

Dr. Laws went on to point out that some of the new research indicates hogs often root up entire young plants to chew on the roots in an attempt to get any nutrients present there.

No-Toes Thompson raised his hand, and was called upon.

"Dr. Laws I've seen places near the bottom of pine trees where it looks like somethin' is rubbin' the bark off. The places don't really look like deer. Could that be hogs?"

"That's very likely. On pines where a good deal of rosin is found, they walk around the entire trunk, pressing their sides against the bark. Most folks think it's to remove ectoparasites from their skin."

"In fact, they will frequently find a tree they really like, and end up rubbing the bark off in a full circle. That's called girdling, and it results in the death of the tree."

Following several additional questions, Murray Laws thoughtfully ended his time at the lectern so the evening's main speaker could come before the group.

>>><<<

Frank Dooley's charge at the Wildlife Marine Resources Department was to begin a study of the wild hog population, and develop strategies to limit

[131]

their rapid population growth. It was a necessity, if the collateral damage to natural, agricultural, and developed property was to be curtailed.

Dooley's comments began by taking his audience back four hundred years, to the 1500's, when Europeans first introduced Eurasian wild boar to North America.

Following the summarized history, he went on to define the term "wild hog" as any free-ranging or wild-living member of the species *Sus scrofa*, to include the Eurasian wild boar, feral hogs, and hybrids between the two.

Toward the end of his comments, Dooley spoke about the anticipated increase in problems associated with wild hogs as their numbers increase exponentially.

He noted that a well-nourished sow could produce two litters a year that average 5.5 (or more) piglets per litter. Such numbers credit a single, healthy female with the ability to produce 110 young per decade. Dooley did the quick math.

"Ladies and gentlemen, twenty females giving birth at that rate would produce 2,200 young in just ten years. Now, that's just 20 sows. Imagine the destructive army 100 females could produce in just one decade!"

"The only precondition being good nutrition, a wild hog is the most prolific large mammal on earth. A population can double in four months.

And, that means we have a problem, a growing problem, here in the Basin, and throughout Coastal Carolina. And, I am confident in predicting it's a problem that will soon spread throughout our state," concluded Dooley.

Waiting to ask a question, several members were about to burst. Again, No-Toes Thompson was the first with his hand in the air. "Mr. Dooley, is there any particular reason why wild pigs adapt so easily to changes in the environment, and reproduce at such a fast rate?"

"Sir, in just two words, I can offer a partial, but very important part of the answer to your question – their gut!"

"They can digest a great variety of food types, which keeps them from becoming tied down to a small geographic area where only one or two types of specific plant matter are found."

"I read of a necropsy recently where almost 20 types of vegetation were found in the stomach of one hog. In addition, there were feathers, mammalian hair, and insect larvae. That variety in acceptable food choice permits the animal to range across a large area, unrestricted by a narrow diet or inefficient digestive system."

Stanford Sparkman, a member from Savannah, asked the next question.

"Frank, what about their breeding habits? Is there seasonality to it?"

"We really don't know for sure, but most feel there is no particular time of the year when breeding occurs more than other times. We know sows come into heat throughout the year, which argues strongly against any real predictability as to when they breed."

Murray Laws may have asked the most pertinent question of the evening.

"Frank, I'd like to ask about their personality, their nature, their temperament. How unnatural do you feel it was for that hog to stop, turn around, and come back to continue the attack on Samantha Wyatt, particularly with Matt Mullinax standing there ready to hit it again with that tree limb?"

"Murray, that's very unusual, to say the least."

"There's no question that wild hogs can be aggressive, particularly when a sow feels her young are threatened. You must remember also, that we're talking about one of the smartest animals you're gonna run up on here in the Basin or anywhere else for that matter. That means they think, they reason, and, if you will, they follow up on their decisions."

"It seems to me; any animal with a set of secondary tusks used for nothing but keeping the primary set razor sharp must be taken seriously."

"And yet, there's really no question the preponderance of our experience is that they prefer to steer clear of humans. Given the opportunity, they will turn and run!"

"That's why it seems to me a reasonable conclusion that you have a non-typical animal on your hands – one that's quite probably smarter than average, clearly more aggressive than average, and plain ol' meaner than average. His actions indicate he's unintimidated by human presence, and that is most unusual."

"Before dinner, a gentleman asked me if I thought this boar was spreading his 'badass genes' around in the swamp."

The round of laughter that followed briefly interrupted Dooley's story.

"Let me answer that question again here at the microphone. Absolutely! And given his reported size and attitude, I'd say any time he takes a notion."

>>><<<

As Frank Dooley was shaking hands, and being thanked by members of the Club, Wartek was following two receptive sows in the upper end of Sumac Swamp.

Before the evening came to a close, Wartek would prove Frank Dooley's comments correct - twice.

[135]

Sixteen

On the Wrong Side of the Creek

Salamander Creek was undistinguished in most respects. However, two things did make the stream a bit out of the ordinary. First, it was rockier than most in the Basin, and second it was home to a large number of black and yellow salamanders – the first distinction contributing to the second.

[136]

Able to hide in the rocks, amphibians and crawfish flourished in the stream's comparatively strong flow. It was a favorite hunting place for raccoons, skunks, weasels, and other small mammals west of Shady River.

But the creek's most significant distinction had to do with the definition of territories in the Basin. The flow formed the southwest boundary of the Thicket Pack's most immediate territory. The group of ferals claimed the creek, and staunchly defended its banks for a mile east and west of their den. The Thicket Pack's position was widely known, and all large, judicious creatures took care in staying well below Salamander Creek.

>>><<<

Though his stride may have appeared otherwise, Seph wasn't hunting. He was taking Aeran on an excursion into the Upper Musclewood Forest. Having waited for cooler weather, it was only the second such trip for the father and son. At 8-months, Aeran was more inquisitive than ever, and his increased stamina helped him keep up with his father. On that afternoon, Seph and Aeran were thoroughly enjoying their romp through the woods.

Twill, Corvin and Gaius' 17-month-old female had come along. She was trotting just off Seph's right hip as he led the trio northwest on the western side of Salamander. Nothing could have been further from the pair's minds than the terror which lay ahead. It would be only a brief lapse in

[137]

concentration, a slight misstep, but it would prove tragic.

"Come on son, keep up with Twill and I. We haven't much daylight remaining."

"I know father, but there's so much to see. I like the water flowing around my legs."

Aeran was a bundle of energy, zigzagging 10 to 15 yards on either side as he ran along behind his father and Twill. He was busy sticking his face into every nook and cranny along the creek banks. Investigating things like an abandoned quail nest, and an impression in the grass where a deer slept the night before were more than Aeran could resist.

The juvenile was every bit his father's son. Seph was small-framed, and at 8-months it was beginning to look as if Aeran would be also. Aeran's ears, tail, and sharply tapered waist mimicked those of his father. In addition, Aeron displayed many of his father's mannerisms. The bond between the two was strong.

When the three dogs reached the fork in Salamander Creek, Seph faced a decision: to continue further northwest into the magnificent tall hardwoods or to turn back toward home.

Seph knew to continue northwest would be to increase the likelihood of an encounter with one or more of the Thicket Pack members. Just being as close to Salamander as they were was of concern. To cross the creek and move along the western edge of the Upper Musclewood Forest would be worse than ill-advised.

>>><<<

It was just such a move years before that led to one of the worst clashes between members of the Thicket and Sandy Knoll Packs.

Seph, Enid and Corvin were little more than adolescent pups when it happened. Neglectfully, four members of the Sandy Knoll troop crossed Salamander Creek, and were jumped by three of the Thicket Pack's largest and fiercest males. It was really no contest.

One Carolina Dog was killed, and left in the edge of the water. Another died the next day at the den. For almost a week following the conflict, keen noses on the Knoll could detect the faint smell of blood in the sand near the water flowing down Salamander.

It was the single worst experience which helped etch a deep-seated fear in the collective mind of the Sandy Knoll Pack – a fear rooted in the realization that Thicket Pack ferals were killers of the first order.

>>><<<

Seph called to Aeran and Twill to turn for home.

The decision was easy, but too long delayed.

The immense Thicket Pack veteran was in full stride when Seph saw him coming. Nolton accelerated at the edge of Salamander Creek. In two leaps he was across, and turning left behind the fleeing pup.

"Run Aeran. Run! Run!" screeched Twill, as she pulled away from Seph, trying to catch Nolton before the giant got to Aeran.

Seph's relatively short legs weren't the only thing churning; his mind was racing also.

Why did I go up the creek? It's so far back down Salamander. He'll never make it back to The Narrows.

Panic filled Seph's mind before the terror found his throat. Barks and whines were followed by what sounded like howls as Seph tried desperately to reach Nolton and Aeran.

>>><<<

The gutsy, black and white Twill was also in hard pursuit. She was something to behold. If Seph could have chosen a Carolina Dog other than one of the fully-grown males to have with him on that fateful day, it would have been Twill.

She was all but fully grown, and more angular than the typical 17-month-old. Her legs were longer, her tail not as curled over her back, her chest broader, and her musculature more developed than other females under two years of age.

Both Corvin and Gaius showed up in their daughter. She had the good looks of her mother and the athletic, sculpted build of her father.

Her piebald markings were no less impressive than those of Corvin, featuring sharp-edged contrast between pure white and deep, rich black.

If her explosive strides could get her to Nolton before he got to Aeran, she could make a difference.

Of course, there was no way Twill could overpower the giant aggressor, but she could distract him enough for Aeran to increase his out-front advantage – an advantage that was clearly shrinking.

With all her power, she pulled with her front and drove with her rear legs as she closed on the large dog with the lion-like mane.

Nolton's strides were longer, but noticeably more lumbering than those of Twill.

Her tongue, waving from the left side of her mouth, the tough-minded female was almost there.

Trailing, but running with all his might, Seph's mind was fixed on the question of Aeran's ability to reach The Narrows, when the young male surprised all three dogs running behind him. About 100 yards above the fork, he turned left across Salamander Creek.

As Aeran made the left turn and reached the western branch, Twill got to Nolton, catching his left rear leg just as he leaned to follow Aeran.

Her momentum took Twill skidding behind and past the big feral, pulling the lion-dog into a stumbling spin to his left. Snarling, growling, doing everything but turning loose, Twill managed to stay on her feet. She continued to back to her right, pulling Nolton in an awkward, skipping, counter-clockwise circle.

Nolton's primary concern was no longer catching the pup, but getting the nasty, Carolina Dog adolescent off his leg. The pain was excruciating.

In a matter of seconds, Seph was into Nolton's right side. He bit hard, with the result being little more than a mouth full of the rogue's reddish-black hair. Nolton swung his powerful head back to the right, sending Seph back-peddling. Aeran's father broke to his right, running in a tight circle around Nolton.

As Twill and his father engaged the lion-dog, Aeran continued across both branches of Salamander Creek, just above the junction. Once across, he turned right and ran south toward the point where Salamander runs into Shady River.

With Nolton licking his ripped ankle, Twill and Seph headed for the crossing at The Narrows, continually looking to their left to see Aeran running just on the other side of Salamander's main flow, hoping to confirm the danger had passed.

Nothing could have been further from the truth!

>>><<<

As Seph ran, his head cleared, and he began to consider the new situation. Aeran was running alone in unquestioned Thicket Pack territory.

"Aeran, get back on this side of the creek. Get back over here with Twill and I. Do it now!" shouted his father. Again, Seph's instructions came too late.

The moments of delay proved tragic.

Forty yards up the incline from the water's edge, none of the Carolina Dogs had seen Thorn running parallel to the earlier chase. Shortly after Aeran crossed at the creek junction and turned south, Thorn began to gradually veer down the gentle slope toward the Carolina pup.

As anger and aggressive impulses grew, he accelerated toward the 8-month-old. Something terrible was going to happen – something fueled by the counsel and examples of Thorn's father.

Exhausted, with eyes fixed on the quickest path through the trees, the pup never saw the beast coming.

Just as he'd done with many smaller animals before, Thorn drove into his victim, with jaws agape and 2-inch canines exposed. He rolled Aeran twice before pinning him down and sinking his teeth into the struggling pup's throat near the base of the jaw. Twice Aeran was lifted from the ground by his head and shaken in the killing vice that was Thorn's jaws.

Seph and Twill were frozen by shock. Once, then a second time Seph started toward his son, only to stop, mortified, and inhibited by the huge feral and unfolding terror on the other side of Salamander Creek.

Aeran kicked several times before coming to rest on his right side, as Thorn continued to bite deeply into Aeran's throat. Thorn's right canine torn into the Carolina youngster's brain stem. That, coupled with the separated windpipe pulled through the large tear in his neck took only moments to kill the young dog.

The massive reddish-brown Rottweiler stood over the body, looking across the creek at Twill and Seph. For a moment there was no movement, only the numbing shock that froze the Carolina Dogs, and the self-satisfied look on Thorn's face.

>>><<<

The trance-like moment was broken when Nolton came charging down Salamander behind Thorn.

Twill and Seph broke for home with Thorn and Nolton running to their left on the opposite side of the creek. It was a strange formation that held together for almost a quarter mile.

Eventually, the two Thicket members bounced to a stop as Seph and Twill neared the place where Salamander merges into Shady River. At The Narrows, Twill led Seph across the river and up the incline toward the den.

During the spring and early summer of 1960, little had been heard from Thorn and the Thicket Pack. That day at Salamander Creek, things changed in a horrific way.

Seventeen

Anger, Anguish and Acceptance

All members knew the heart-wrenching loss of Aeran was not the first time Seph and Bedwyr had grieved deeply. The earlier loss of a son at birth, and the mysterious disappearance of a daughter were both very difficult.

The difference following Salamander Creek was Seph, who blamed himself for Aeran's death. During the first week following Thorn's attack, he was inconsolable. Even Bedwyr was beginning to re-group and move on, as her mate struggled with deep, gnawing depression.

Enid, Bree, Corvin, Gaius, and the 17-month-olds, Gwain and Twill, had joined Bedwyr in trying to see Seph through his grief, all to no avail.

On the evening of the 7th day after the tragedy, Twill moved close to Seph at the back of the large common room. She was going to make her most determined effort to reason with Tesha's father, a respected long-time elder in the group.

Having been there, her perspective on what happened was more informed than other Pack members. She hoped that would lend weight to her words.

"Seph, if you are responsible for what happened to Aeran, then so am I. I should have run the giant down, and stopped him in his tracks. I should have had a vision of Thorn running through the woods. I should have sat Aeran down before things began, and explained the danger across that creek. I should have intercepted Thorn's charge, and sent him running for home with my overpowering strength."

"I should have done all these things, but I was able to do none! I did all that I could do, and that's what helps heal my heart," whispered Twill with lips only a short distance from Seph's ear.

Seph blinked twice, as Twill continued.

"In truth, you were no more capable of doing any of those things than was I. You did what you could do in trying to stop the lion-dog's attack. The fact is, if you had crossed that creek to confront Thorn, you would have died too!"

"I was there, and I know my words are true!"

"Tesha and Bedwyr need you! The Pack needs you! There is danger around us. Not one of us doubts your courage, and we all want you back with us!"

Corvin, Enid, and Bedwyr were sitting nearby as Twill spoke.

"Her words are true Seph. Heed them and let's begin to deal with the challenge we face," said Corvin.

"How do you know what I feel, Corvin? You didn't watch your son die! I have a right to my grief," replied Seph, as he pushed up to a sitting position.

That was the moment Enid chose to speak – thoughtfully, but with resolve.

"Listen to me Seph. Following Aeran's death, the only guilt you will bear will be if you fail to be what you are...a responsible, contributing elder in this Pack."

"That attack could have come many places in the Musclewood, not just at Salamander Creek. The monster has even come to our den in hopes of killing us. The responsibility you must face is tied to the future, not the past. You must gather and refocus your thoughts. You must help us do what we must do – protect our home and our loved ones."

"Stop the self-pity and show some strength! Be assured, I speak for all of us, including your mate, Bedwyr, and your beautiful daughter, Tesha!"

Seph was struck by the directness and undeniable truth of Enid's words. He made no response. But at that moment, Enid managed to fashion a new perspective in the thinking of his long-time companion.

The next morning, outside the den, Seph walked up to Enid and offered his simple reply: "Thank you."

Later in the day Enid saw Seph and Bedwyr running around the base of a tree, as they'd done several weeks before Aeran's death. There were indications another litter of pups was on the way.

Eighteen

No Typical Hog Hunt, No Typical Hog

With the exception of a week's worth of staking out corn piles, the club's first serious attempt to kill the dangerous boar involved six hunters and four dogs.

The hunters included:

...Stanford Sparkman, a successful electrical contractor from Savannah;

...Club President Clinton Dunlap;

...storied hunters, Adam and Art Nutter from Pooler, GA;

...Hershel Loflin, an airline pilot from Charleston, SC, and

...Charlene Garrett, a retired Banker from Swainsboro, GA.

[150]

All were members of the Club except Art and Adam Nutter. They were experienced hunters of all things big, hairy, and dangerous. The tougher the job and rougher the terrain, the more the identical twins liked it. Working in the woods all their lives, they'd grown up in the family logging business. Their reputations were well established.

One of the better stories that followed the Nutters concerned Art. It was reported that on one occasion he walked up to a disc of upturned roots at the base of a large, fallen tree. The root formation partially covered the entrance to a bobcat's den. The story went that just as Art bent over to check it out, the panicked cat ran for daylight. The scars in several places convinced most that Art had in fact been successful in killing the cat with his bare hands and a pocket knife.

As confirmation, the large, yellow and black cat had been mounted and put on display in the Nutter Logging Services offices for all to see.

All six hunters had entered the woods many times in pursuit of large game – deer, bear, elk and even mountain lion hunts were on their resumes. However, the hunters were only slightly more impressive than the dogs they owned.

>>><<<

Ernest and Hemingway were magnificent hounds. Ernest was a classically-built black and tan. Hemingway was an award-winning bloodhound, as were his father and grandfather.

Both had won national honors. Although none had been garnered nationally, Hemingway had taken top spot in several regional dog shows.

Their well-to-do owner, Charlene Garrett, was one of the club's early hog hunting fans, as well as a committed reader of America's famous authors. The two hounds on that day's hunt shared a pen back home with Mark and Twain.

Often hunting hogs with her husband before his untimely death, Charlene was as committed and durable as any of the club's male members. She was a regular on the Wyoming and Georgia trips.

The other two dogs everyone hoped would help flush the huge hog were owned by the twins from South Georgia. Puddin was a larger-than-average male Irish terrier, and the other male, Pie, most nearly favored an American bulldog, with his broad face and squared-off chest.

Puddin and Pie weren't as experienced as Ernest and Hemingway, but they were every bit as strong and gritty. All four dogs were well-conditioned, clear-eyed, and individually striking.

A competition between the owners was inevitable as to which pair would be first to engage Wartek. However, had they known the full extent of the giant boar's power and threat, they may well have been less enthusiastic about urging their dogs into the fray.

>>><<<

Stanford Sparkman and Clinton Dunlap loaded up with Charlene Garrett for the 10-minute ride up County Route 1102. They planned to enter the forest and work their way south into the Sumac.

One assumption had been made. In the middle of the day, if you want to find the biggest and badest, you go to the swamp's wettest and worst. That's where the dogs came in. After providing a basic heading, the hunters planned to let the canines do the work of finding and flushing Wartek. It was very likely his location would be in one of the Sumac's most inaccessible areas.

Of course, each hunter knew the trick was going to be helping the dogs locate the right spot and corner the right animal. That task, as much as anything, would require some 18-karat luck.

The Nutters and Hershel Loflin moved northwest from the hunting lodge, and entered the southern end of the swamp. They were going to head for the spot where Shady Spur and Shady River merged.

They had no way of knowing their target was where he usually stayed – the wet, triangular-shaped area below the divide in West Horney Head Creek.

As things were shaping up, it looked as though Puddin and Pie would be closest to Wartek, and likely have first shot at bringing the Sumac titan to bay. Of course, when it came to Wartek, how things seemed to be, and how they worked out were often very different.

>>><<<

As they entered the woods, Loflin was walking a short distance behind the Nutters. Cranked up and ready to go, Puddin and Pie were lunging against the leash, jumping forward on their hind legs almost as much as they were walking.

Neither Hershel nor anyone else in the Club had met the Nutter boys before the morning of the hunt. The club's recent guest speaker, Frank Dooley, had arranged for the Georgia duo to help in doing away with the rogue boar.

As he followed them deeper into the woods, the veteran commercial pilot couldn't help studying his companions.

Both stood six foot five, and weighted in north of 300 pounds. Each had a full beard that reached his chest. From the top of their sideburns, the Nutters kept their heads shaved completely bald.

Art was marginally the heavier of the two, but he and Adam were very muscular. Both wore overalls and boots of World War II vintage. When the two walked up, what really turned folks' eye was the content of Adam's shoulder holster – a highly polished .357 Magnum with a 6 and ¾ inch barrel.

The hand gun and cartridge had been around for 25 years, but in 1960 it was still a rare weapon to see, especially one with so impressive a barrel and finish.

Art's pants were tucked into the full, lace-up boots just below the knee. All he wore above his handmade belt was a black leather vest, with an embroidered profile of the world's ugliest boar on the back. His .45 caliber pistol was dwarfed by the heavy, bone-handled machete hanging on his right side.

"Art, you guys never carry rifles on these hunts?" asked Hershel.

"No, hopefully the dogs can back 'em in a hole, and let us get close enough to use the handgun or maybe the machete. We let you guys with the heavy-duty firepower take the long range shots. We think of our job as helping our clients get that opportunity."

"Well, I'll tell ya. I believe you fellas are just the ones to do that....you two, along with Puddin and Pie, of course."

The three walked several yards further before Loflin spoke again.

"Guys, I've got another question, if you don't mind."

"Certainly Mr. Loflin," replied Art.

"Knowing wild hogs are most active at night, why are we hunting in the middle of the day?"

"Mr. Loflin, you're correct. Wild hogs are nocturnal. For the most part, they are indeed most active from just before sundown to just after sunrise. During the middle of the day they tend to stay in or near the wettest, coolest, and thickest parts of the swamp. That makes it easier for us and the dogs to focus on a particular place, rather than trying to intercept them on the fly," explained Art.

It was strange to see the Nutter twins in their singular, somewhat outlandish garb, and then hear them speak so eloquently. Many would not suspect, but both held degrees in Forestry. Art, the oldest by less than two minutes, had gone on to earn his Master's from the University of Florida.

>>><<<

Two minutes into the woods, and the four dogs were running. Hemingway was the first to find hogs. He was soon joined by Ernest in backing a sizable sow and four adolescents into a mud hole just off County Route 1102.

Matt Mullinax had provided a clear description of the jumbo porker they were hunting – huge head and shoulders, long wrinkled snout, flared tusks more straight than curved, rust coloration with irregular black patches, and what he thought was a missing or sharply folded-over top of his left ear.

As they neared the action, Charlene could see the sow wasn't the intended target.

[156]

It took three blasts on the whistle before Ernest and Hemingway backed off and returned to their owner. As with all hunters watching quality dog's work for the first time, Clinton Dunlap and Stan Sparkman were more than impressed. The hounds may have been surprised by the early whistle, but they knew just what it meant. As always, they responded in short order, coming directly to their owner.

After walking a hundred yards on down the eastern branch of Horney Head, Charlene again sent the hounds to the right and into the swamp.

>>><<<

As the Garrett dogs worked, Hershel Loflin and the Nutter twins followed Puddin and Pie to the eastern Horney Head before turning north. The dogs crossed the creek, and began working in ankle-deep water. The Piedmont Airlines pilot knew from the outset that his conditioning would be put to the test. The Nutter twins jogged as much or more than they walked.

Pie was the first to really cut loose. He was near the triangular-shaped section of land formed by the secondary fork in West Horney Head – home to several of Wartek's favorite wallows.

"Come on, let's go! He's got something!" shouted Art. That's when Puddin chimed in. The duo's barks and howls were soon rivaled by the frantic squeals and grunts of wild hogs.

[157]

From mountain lions to eastern cottontails, when pursuing hounds strike a trail, there's a tonal change that perks up the hunter's ear.

Puddin and Pie's participation in a canine-hog chorale was likely the only time the Nutters welcomed the screechy, off-key complaints of wild hogs. The twins, fully focused on the hunt, managed a smile as they splashed through the standing water listening to their dogs' vocalizations coming through the woods.

When the Nutters and Loflin arrived, the dogs were well into a confrontation with three boars and one wet sow.

One of the two larger hogs at the head of the defensive formation was Ezy, bouncing on his front legs, throwing his head into the air, and seeming to dare the Nutter dogs to come deeper into the muddy hole.

Come on in here dog! Come closer to me, and I'll end your days with my tusks!

Ezy wasn't Wartek, but he was a large, nasty customer. More than once he'd gone to school on Wartek's daunting displays, and his frequently-lethal follow through.

One real slip and either dog would know the agony of deep, life-threatening gashes at the ends of Ezy's tusks.

The twins were well aware of the danger as well. Both had pulled their pistols and stood at the ready.

Puddin swung around to the right, and cut across the incline above the large mud hole. His intent was to outflank the hogs, but the second boar moved to intercept him Puddin's right front leg slipped under him, putting the terrier on his right side. The boar charged, driving a tusk into the terrier's left shoulder.

Puddin's panicked, high-pitched whine was immediately followed by the roar of Adam Nutter's shiny .357. The offending hog dropped on his right side like his legs had been cut from under him.

Ezy and the remaining swine bolted, and disappeared in several directions out the back side of the wallow.

"How bad is it Adam," asked Art as his brother knelt over the bleeding dog.

"Can't tell for sure, but it definitely ain't good."

Adam was particularly close to the red terrier. As they traveled from one hunt to another, he often found himself stroking Puddin's mustache and goatee. Puddin had been hunting with the Nutter twins for just over six years, and had come to be Adam's favorite among their five dogs.

Adam picked up the injured hunter, and carried him all the way back to the truck. Puddin would survive, but for that day the Nutter dogs' hunt was over.

Twenty minutes sooner and they would have found Wartek with the other hogs in the wallow. He'd heard the earlier cries of the sow and Charlene's bellowing hounds. When the whistle split the air, Wartek began his stiff-legged strut up Horney Head Creek.

In his territory, the bad boar stood far apart from the crowd. Almost always, he chose to head toward a ruckus, not away from it.

>>><<<

Charlene Garrett's dogs had gotten further ahead than she liked. When in a swamp, she much

[160]

preferred they work where she could see their movements. Chest-deep muck could change the odds, and do so very quickly. Coon hunters were well aware of what the water could do to help a raccoon drown a larger and stronger dog. Similar dynamics were possible when a wild hog, much more accustomed to life in the sticky wetlands, took on a hunting dog in shoulder-deep water. Raccoons used nimble fingers and disproportionately strong hands to hold the dog's head under water, while wild hogs often drove sharp tusks up from under the flailing dog.

Charlene's rule was simple: as best you can, keep your animals in sight and your hand on your weapon. That's why she carried her husband's .45 ACP, along with an 8-inch blade. And, of course, there was always that cattle prod strung over her left shoulder.

"Here now Hemmy. Come here Ernie! Come here you two. Ernest, Hemingway, come here!" Sparkman and Dunlap stood just behind Charlene as she called out for a second time.

Next she placed a finger to each corner of her mouth, and issued a whistle shriller than the one produced by the stainless steel referee's model hanging around her neck. There was no response. The silence had gone on far longer than she liked. It was alarming, and growing more so with each passing second.

[161]

At last there came a single slow, low-key bellow, followed by two throaty barks.

"That was Ernest. Something's wrong!" yelled Charlene, as she ran across Horney Head and into the thicker slough on the other side. Sparkman and Dunlap were close behind.

Only one more bark was heard from Ernie, but it was enough to redirect Charlene toward his location. When she got to him, the black and tan was standing in water that reached the base of his neck.

As best she could, Garrett gave him a quick onceover. There was no blood – no injuries she could feel or see. Next she surveyed the area, but saw nothing.

"Ernie, where's Hemingway? Where is he big boy?" asked Charlene as she stroked the hound's head.

The recently-retired banker stood and slipped her fingers under Ernest's collar. As she turned to lead him back toward Sparkman and Dunlap, the black and tan pulled away, and went several steps beyond where he had been standing. When Charlene followed, she was jolted by what she saw – reddish-black hair and a white paw just below the surface.

"No! No! Oh God, please no!" screamed Hemingway's owner, as she wrapped her right arm around the chest of the submerged bloodhound.

Stan Sparkman struggled to hurry his legs through the knee-deep water.

Charlene stumbled twice as she and Sparkman struggled to carry Hemingway to a spot where the watery muck was shallower. The black and tan was right behind, sniffing at the tip of his hunting partner's tail.

Charlene finally got the dog's body to a small hammock rising a few inches above the water's surface. Her trembling was so intense she could barely stand. On the hammock, just above the water's surface, is where the three hunters saw the extent of Hemingway's injuries. Charlene Stovall Garrett was a tough lady, but what she saw brought wails and tears as she fell to her knees.

A large piece of skin and muscle on the right side of Hemingway's face had been sliced from the jawbone and skull. The bone glistened as a small amount of blood continued to bead at the edge of the gash, outlining the oval-shaped wound.

There were grotesque, grinding, wounds at the back of Hemingway's neck. The tissue and hair was wadded like a macabre, mound of meatloaf. Stan Sparkman's eyes and thoughts were drawn there.

Bits of flesh remained entangled with the wads of hair pulled from the dog's neck.

"What in God's name happened to the back of his neck?" whispered Clinton Dunlap.

[163]

Two punctures in Hemingway's chest trailed several inches upward into the hollow of his neck. Most distressing of all was the large laceration beginning in the middle of the dog's stomach and extending to the groin muscles.

Along with sudden and severe blood loss, the long belly-wound had resulted in disembowelment from the bottom of the hound's sternum to the front of his left rear leg.

The creamy, pink and bluish bowels inside the body lining stood in stark contrast to the dark color of Hemingway's heavy, matted coat. The scene was horrendous in every sense of the word. Blood continued to seep from clusters of small capillaries in and near the cuts in the body wall.

All had been in the woods many times and listened to more than their share of deep woods hunting stories. But never had they seen or heard of such damage to a strong and experienced hunting dog, of any kind.

>>><<<

Ernest stepped away and laid down several yards away as Charlene Garrett and the two men eased Hemingway down. The big black and tan opted not to look at Hemingway's body in such horrid condition. As was his owner, Ernest was trembling and whining softly.

Remarkably, there'd been no barking to bring the hound running early in the attack. When he realized what was going on, he was simply unable to close the distance between himself and Hemingway before the killer hog was going out the opposite side of the chest-deep water.

As the hunters knelt over Hemingway's body, Wartek looked unnatural, standing less than forty yards away, watching and relishing the moment.

As he scrubbed his tongue against the roof of his mouth, dissolving what remained of the dog's blood, he again demonstrated his most befuddling trait, remaining nearby, rather than fleeing any continuing threat the Obtruders might pose.

Nineteen

Expert Testimony

No one involved knew for sure if the boar that attacked Samantha Wyatt was the same animal that killed Charlene Garrett's bloodhound, but it seemed a reasonable conclusion.

How likely could it have been that two huge, outrageously aggressive hogs strong and quick enough to take down an experienced dog like Hemingway would be in the same area at the same time? It was highly unlikely; particularly when you consider the even more remote possibility they would tolerate one another's presence.

>>><<<

Three days later, six club members met at Alex's Diner to talk about the events on Horney Head Creek.

Dr. Shane Pascal, a local, well-respected veterinarian was invited to join the group. He had examined Hemingway, and wanted to share his finding with the group.

"I don't want to come across like some crime show criminal pathologists here, but I tried to take a close look at Hemingway before preparing my notes. I've never seen anything like it," said Pascal, before pausing to take a sip of coffee.

"The slicing and partial tearing on the side of Hemingway's head not only took away much of the muscle and scalp around the ear, but the gouging dislocated his jaw. To do that took a lot of strength, a very violent assault, plus long, sharp tusks."

Every eye at the table was fixed on Pascal. Each listener hung on his every word. The subject was proving unnerving, as well as fascinating.

"You know, the terrible damage done to his head or even the deep puncture wounds in his chest would have likely proven fatal," said the vet as he stared at the bottom of his half-empty coffee cup. His words had a thinking-out-loud quality to them.

[167]

"Why would the hog prolong an attack that surely was proving both overpowering and fatal shortly after it began?" pondered Pascal, before sitting up straight and hesitating again for the waitress to refill his cup.

Before he could continue, Hemingway's owner eased forward in her chair to ask a question. "Dr. Pascal, you're implying something like overkill? Is that what we're looking at here?"

"Well, I'm not sure, Charlene. But it does seem likely to me that inflicting such damage would have proven sufficient to send any wild hog fleeing from such an encounter. Hemingway would clearly have been down, and the hog could have reasonably felt he'd more than made his point. I would think the animal would've concluded it was time to get while the gettin' was good. But...but, I think this guy stayed around a while."

"What makes you think that Shane?" asked Stanford Sparkman?

"There were marks at the base of the skull that looked like the hog chewed, not a bite here and there mind you, but *chewed* on Hemingway for a period of time. The wounds wouldn't have been so extensive and concentrated, if Hemingway had still been alive and resisting."

Charlene pushed back in her chair, lowered and slowly shook her head.

"I know this is hard to hear. We can certainly change the subject," said Clinton Dunlap as he rested his hand on Charlene's forearm.

"No. I want to know what happened, and just how that bastard so quickly and easily got the best of a very, very good dog."

It was creepy to hear Pascal's description of what happened to Hemingway. Everyone began to develop a mental image of the hog as some silk-caped villain, defying all the rules of wild hog behavior. However, that's exactly how it sounded.

"So, what have we got here, Dr. Pascal?" asked Adam Nutter, who until that point had been noticeably silent.

"You make it sound like this critter fears neither man nor beast, and behaves more like some Jack the Ripper than a big bad boar....which is all he is."

"Mr. Nutter, according to everything I've read and heard, all I'm saying is that's it's very unusual, very, very unusual, for a wild hog of any size to be as aggressive and confrontational as this animal appears to have been in this conflict."

"He looks to have not only tried to gnaw the dog's head off, it looks to me like the long laceration to the underbelly happened postmortem. He disemboweled the bloodhound after it was already dead."

[169]

"My God Shane, what makes you think that," ask Clinton Dunlap, pushing back against the edge of the table.

"Clinton, the cut was made in almost a single, long motion. There were no indications of stops and starts along the edges of the cut in the body wall. Nor were there discrete stabbing wounds in the intestines themselves. You would see those if Hemingway had been opened up by the violent up and down motion of a hog thrusting and withdrawing in an on-going struggle."

There was nothing but silence, before the veterinarian turned again to Garrett.

"Charlene, that's why I answered your earlier question about overkill like I did – I'm not sure."

"If the hog knew Hemingway was down for the count, opening him up like that would seem more like plain old morbid cruelty than anything else."

Everyone around the table was dealing with their own thoughts when the waitress returned with a fresh pot of coffee. There were no takers.

With most still staring at the table, Pascal continued.

"I've run my thoughts by several people who know much more about wild hog behavior than I do. They all agree; things add up to an animal that operates outside typical bounds – an animal that needs to be removed. And I'm thinkin' that's going to be easier said than done."

>>><<<

It was Adam Nutter that broke the next silence.

"Thank God we didn't lose a dog like Ms. Garrett did, but I've got one badly hobbled-up after only one trip into that swamp. That's why Art and I are up to gettin' back in there, and finishing the job. If the Club is ready to host another hunt, we're in. We'll kill that bastard!"

Dr. Pascal raised his right hand and index finger in a just-one-more-thing gesture.

"Folks, there's something else I'd like to mention. For me it makes the image of that fight in the swamp even more puzzling – almost unbelievable."

"I couldn't find any wild hog hairs in Hemingway's mouth – not a single one under the lips, around the gums, on the tongue or in the throat – not one!"

"It looks to me like Hemingway didn't get his teeth into the hog a single time. How likely is that – a big hog, probably not stopped, but likely slowed by the deep water, and an experienced, powerful hunting dog like Hemingway doesn't get his teeth into him a single time? Could that be?"

Again, the attendees expressed their surprise with their silence. Hearing that the evidence

[171]

showed Hemingway was unsuccessful at putting up the most basic resistance compounded the shock-value of Shane Pascal's report.

"God Almighty, what sort of animal do we have on our hands here?" asked Charlene Garrett, expressing alarm rather than seeking an answer.

"Mrs. Garrett, Mr. Nutter was right; he's only a big, bad boar – but likely a boar that's as mean and bloodthirsty as you'll ever see. After hearing what he did to the Wyatt girl, and spending two hours going over the body of that bloodhound, I'd say do away with him...the best way you can as soon as you can...kill him!"

The Veterinarian's words might have struck some as overly dramatic, but no one at the table took them for granted.

>>><<<

"I can assure you the Shady River Hunting Club has every intention of finishing what that boar has started. Twice as many hunters have called about going next time," announced Clinton Dunlap.

With the exception of Charlene Garrett, all the other breakfast meeting attendees expressed the same interest.

"Gentlemen, I'm afraid this time I'm going to pass. One dead dog is enough for me. I hope you all understand."

Everyone did.

[172]

As the meeting broke up, each expressed appreciation for her participation in round one. The first gut-check in the lower end of Shady River Basin was over.

The Obtruders planned to go in force, and the objective was simple – the end of Wartek's reign.

Twenty
A Reasoned Response

As troublesome as developments on the first hunt were for members of the Hunt Club, they couldn't compare with the trauma on Sandy Knoll.

The terrible loss of Aeran and the re-emergence of Thicket Pack violence had left all the Carolina Dogs deeply distressed.

Discussion of retaliation options were held among all Pack members, and on several occasions just among the Carolina males.

It was one of the entire-pack meetings where Enid first began to speak directly to a need for patient and careful planning. None of the Knoll Pack reacted with more anger to Enid's arguments for a measured response than Seph.

"I want to kill the Thicket Pack, every one of them! That's my position, Enid!"

"Why do you always argue for caution rather than courage? Why do you portray our strengths as limited, and speak of our weakness as the prime concern?" asked Seph angrily.

Enid and Bree's four pups gathered in one of the rear chambers. Tesha had already slipped into the hiding space behind the large roots in the front chamber. The Pack's youngest members were unaccustomed to extended days of tension among the adults, especially between Enid and Corvin.

"I would like to hear that answer as well, Enid. It does seem like your counsel always calls for restraint," added Corvin.

"I'm not speaking of restraint, but of reason. I'm not asking that we be guided by a fear of failure, but by a plan informed by facts."

"Today, we know taking on the Thicket Pack is to take on the giant Thorn and his powerful bitch, Gwenfar. Then there is the evil-eyed Novic and Chesman".

"With the exception of Chesman, eye-to-eye, we are out-weighted and less powerful than Thicket Pack members."

"Who among us can overpower and kill Thorn? And, what about the lion-dog, Nolton? The brave and proud fighter, Captain, is no longer among us. He would quickly have agreed to fight Thorn or Nolton.....and he would have died. Should I accept the same challenge, who hear truly believes I would escape the same fate?"

"Perhaps we could send Seph against the lion again. Seph, you and every member of our Pack know he is fully the threat he has always been. Twill is right; if you had crossed that creek in an attempt to save Aeran, Thorn or Nolton, perhaps both would have killed you too."

[175]

"Our plan must be more than an attack fueled only by rage and revenge. We must hope for some good fortune to turn things more in our favor!"

"What good fortune are you talking about, Enid? What is it you expect to happen that will help us defeat the monsters in the thicket?" asked Mace.

"At this moment, I don't know what specific events might provide an advantage, what circumstances may come about that would turn the odds more in our favor. But I do know this...if we take on the Thicket Pack as things currently stand, we will likely lose all we hold dear!"

There were several moments of silence.

"My friends, make no mistake! I favor a strong response – one that spills Thicket Pack blood. But not at the risk of destroying our Pack."

"It's my intention to lead us with a plan that destroys Thorn's group, and rids the Basin of their wickedness, forever. But rushing into a foolish, ill-conceived confrontation is not the way!"

"We all must understand something else as well. Whatever we do, it will not be without risk and the chance of failure. Think carefully. This will require commitment to see it through, and each member will have to do their part."

>>><<<

A second gut-check in the Musclewood was complete. The Carolina Dogs committed to following Enid's lead in dealing with the Thicket Pack threat.

Unknown to Enid, his plan would in fact be aided by the good fortune he'd referenced – good fortune in the form of a shocking turn of events.

Twenty-One
Introducing Renshaw

Not since the fatal attack on Aeran had the Thicket Pack threatened the Carolina Dogs. Only once since Aeran's death had the groups' paths crossed. That occurred when Mace saw Chesman chasing a muskrat on the far side of The Narrows.

The Thicket Pack membership was stable, consisting of the mated pairs, Thorn and Gwenfar and Chesman and Izepha, along with two unmated males, Novic and Nolton. On the membership front there had been only one development. It was a new arrival working hard to gain full acceptance. The newcomer was a handsome, short-haired German pointer named Renshaw.

The pointer had known both good and bad times in the past. He'd received impeccable training and excellent treatment from his long-time breeder/owner, but it was a different story with the family that bought him before his breeder retired and moved to Arizona. Neglected and physically abused, Renshaw ran for freedom at his first opportunity.

>>><<<

Before coming to the Thicket Pack's immediate territory, Renshaw had been on his own for fourteen months, trying to master life in the wild. He'd made progress, but the transition from

[178]

bagged food poured in a bowl to small mammals, and, at times, carrion, was trying his very fiber. At one point, he almost died of starvation before an otter hit by a car provided a much-needed meal.

At a kill where the Pack took a large doe and didn't fully consumer it, Renshaw was able to eat his fill. From that point on, the intelligent pointer understood what "grist of the group" meant when it came to survival in the wild.

By the 1st of November, he was permitted to sleep near, but not directly under the huge rock that covered the Pack's hollowed-out den. Thorn continued to forbid an inclusive sleeping place, even though other Pack members were impressed with the new arrival's remarkable sense of smell and tracking prowess.

>>><<<

Looking to her left at the pointer curled up near the base of a black gum tree, Gwenfar stood up and moved toward Thorn.

"When will Renshaw be permitted to sleep closer?" she asked.

Thorn neither raised his head nor offered a response. The question, indeed the entire subject didn't hold great priority for the Thicket Pack leader. His acquiescence on the matter could come sooner, or it could come later. He felt no responsibility for Renshaw's burden with the continuing state of limbo.

[179]

"Please Thorn, can we talk about this?"

"Why are you so concerned, Gwenfar?" snapped Thorn.

"I think his interest in joining us is sincere, and I have heard Nolton and Novic speak well of his hunting skills. You also have said he's a good hunter. We could use him. Everyone knows our numbers are not as great as they used to be."

"Thorn, I hope you will decide to let him join us," concluded Gwenfar before moving back to the other side of the resting area.

Thorn's mate wasn't sharing everything that motivated her request.

Two weeks earlier, Izepha, her brother's mate and Gwenfar's closest companion, shared with Gwenfar a secret that would likely disrupt the Pack. The pups Izepha was carrying had not been fathered by Chesman, but by the newly-arrived red and white German pointer, Renshaw.

Twenty-Two

Curiosity Killed the Coyote

Only once had the coyotes across Shady River attempted to harm Ingrum and his family – only once, but the effort was nearly a disaster.

Pixlee and her pups were outside the den, 20 feet from safety when Cunea started her charge. The first pup was successful with a dash through the triangular opening at the base of the rocks. But the second was farther away, and in more danger as the attack began.

Ingrum's mate charged the coyote in an attempt to give the second kit time to reach the den entrance. She was successful, but paid the price of a badly-bitten foreleg. The female coyote withdrew just long enough for Ingrum's mate to get back under the rocks that sheltered the den.

The determined female then forced her head, and most of her shoulders into the opening, where Ingrum was waiting with a wicked bite to her nose.

Cunea withdrew from the opening to lower her head and drag the inside of her right foreleg across the tip of her bleeding nose.

Lodren was standing just outside.

"As I asked, you should have waited for me, Cunea. I could have blocked their retreat. We would have enjoyed fresh meat, and you wouldn't have a sore nose," said Lodren as the pair turned toward home.

"Lodren, I was hungry and you were late!" replied Cunea, glancing over at her smaller mate. A few more strides and she expressed something else that seemed always on the tip of her tongue.

"And whose idea was it to come this far from home in the first place?" she asked, shaking blood from the wound at the end of her muzzle. Lodren readily understood his mate was making a statement as much as asking a question.

"As I recall, the decision was made jointly," retorted Lodren

The truth was, Lodren was beginning to second-guess the decision as well. Much of the surrounding area was wetter than Cunea and Lodren would have preferred. In addition, two skirmishes with the Shady Knoll Pack had further soured their first few weeks in the Basin. Both cocky coyotes were dealing with the fact they were no match for the Carolina Dogs.

With the failure to snatch one or both of the fox pups, Cunea and Lodren had to continue the morning hunt. Their efforts the previous afternoon and evening produced only one small rabbit and two field mice. Both were hungry.

>>><<<

In just under an hour, they were at one of their favorite hunting places – the area north of Shady Spur. In addition to the squirrels, rabbits, waterfowl and other more routine prey, the Spur offered an opportunity to enjoy two items from the specialty menu.

Cunea brought an acquired taste with her from northeast Louisiana – crawfish. With mid-sized and larger individuals, she'd learned to separate the abdomen from the front part of the body, and extract the pleasing muscle meat from the tail. It was a taste and technique Lodren hadn't mastered. However, that morning the growls in his stomach motivated his interest in giving it another try.

As with Cunea and the freshwater crustacean, Lodren had acquired a new taste of his own since arriving in the Basin – box turtles. He'd discovered just how easy it was to turn a box turtle into boxed lunch.

From their youngest days, box turtles face the onslaught of various Basin predators. Birds, weasels, raccoons, skunks, wild hogs, turkeys, possums, cats, snakes, and dogs snacked on the small reptiles. Even other box turtles took advantage of smaller turtles' very soft shell.

As with all predators, the easily-opened shell was the reason Lodren found box turtles a quick and satisfying meal. It didn't fully harden until they were 7-years-old. In fact, the hinge to the protective shell door didn't develop until the turtle reached 2-years. Tearing them open was no problem for a sharp-toothed, hungry coyote. The waters of Shady Spur offered large numbers of the turtle with the brown and yellow shell.

There was one particular practice which proved troubling to many observers when canine predators made a meal of box turtles. They chewed off the legs before pulling open the shell. It was a macabre appetizer also enjoyed by the coyotes.

>>><<<

Cunea was looking for crawfish, and her mate was scouring the banks for turtles, when Lodren first detected the smell. The scent was faint but distinct – flesh, more aged than spoiled. Lodren's attention was instantly drawn away from the banks and his search for turtles.

The compact male raised his head and filled his nose again. This time the picture his nostrils painted was clearer, and the meal they described even larger and more appealing.

"Cunea, test the air!" said Lodren, again moving his head from side to side, trying to sharpen his interpretation of the smell filling his nose.

Cunea raised her head and promptly found the scent. She too knew a meal was nearby, but her choice was to continue uncovering the plump crawfish hiding at her feet.

"You do smell that, don't you?"

His mate didn't respond as Lodren stepped out of the water and headed down the creek. Again, he drew in the breeze, and again the message was clear – the strong smell of meat and the equally-strong possibility of a full belly.

"Come on, Cunea. Let's go see what that's all about," called Lodren, briefly looking back at the female as he increased his pace. Cunea never even looked in her mate's direction, the last opportunity she would have to do so.

>>><<<

Perhaps she would have followed, had she known the short distance required to reach the feast – a feast far exceeding a week's worth of turtle or a month's worth of crawfish.

Lodren needed to round only two bends in Shady Spur, and go a short 30 yards into the woods to discover the source of the tantalizing smell.

Difficult to see at first, his nose took the coyote to a large mound of pine needles, dirt-covered leaves and sticks. Drawing close, he could make out the figure of a whitetail under the debris, a large doe.

Pawing away portions of the cover, Lodren saw that a portion of the neck, entire right shoulder and most of the organs were gone. The animal appeared to have been killed and fed upon the previous night.

As he stood over the carcass, a small switch went on in the back of his head – a vague recollection that seemed as much a moment in a dream as a specific memory from the past. He tried to recall the occasion from his earliest days, when his father offered counsel about such a scene.

He said I must be aware when this is found. It's unnatural. It comes with danger. He said others had been here and would return.

Lodren looked in all directions, but his empty stomach spoke louder than his father's unfocused words from the past.

>>><<<

Standing behind the doe, he began to pull up and back on the skin just above the large hole that

[186]

had been eaten out of the right shoulder. His efforts revealed a still-red cylinder of muscle running along the right side of the backbone.

His meal got no further than a single tug on the exposed, lengthy loin.

Steed was the first to get to the coyote. His brief crouching stalk, soft-footed acceleration, and pounce came without Lodren even knowing another predator was near. In fact, there were two watching over their kill from cover a few dozen yards away.

As Steed wrapped his front legs around Lodren's chest, dug his claws into both sides of the coyote's underbelly, and sunk his teeth into the back of Lodren's head, Tally drug her claws down the top of the canine's back. The sharp points dug in at the back of his rump, stripping skin and fur from the top half of the coyote's tail.

Once driven to the ground, Lodren never got back to his feet.

"Cunea, Cunea please help, Cunea!" shouted Lodren to his mate, who was already in a desperate sprint toward the loud growls. Larger, heavier, and more aggressive than typical females, Cunea had always been protective of Lodren.

In this case however, her attempt at rescue would prove the gravest of mistakes.

By the time she rounded the second bend in the creek and turned right into the woods, there was nothing that could be done for Lodren.

>>><<<

Not only was her arrival too late for her curious mate, the sprint brought her to within ten feet of the tensed, crouching Malya.

Cunea was able to make only a slight turn to her left before Malya was in full control. The savage cat needed no help to quickly subdue and kill the struggling female coyote.

Once stilled, for no apparent reason other than arrogance and self-regard, Malya lifted the front half of Cunea's body, and swung the dead coyote from side to side. Carrying Cunea so only her rear paws and the tip of her tail drug the ground, Malya walked toward the place where Steed lay with both front legs across Lodren's body.

>>><<<

Even though she appeared the essence of confidence in dropping the dead canine at Tally's feet, returning to the doe, and licking back skin to expose more meat, there was a disturbing internal conflict growing in the cubs' mother.

For several months two realities had persistently racked Malya's mind, and the time to face both was near.

Twenty-Three

Sudden Separation

In her adult years, Malya had delivered three litters, all born in the spring. The first consisted of two males, each living well beyond the point where they left Malya's care to undertake life on their own.

Overly cautious when she was younger, Malya moved her first two cubs three times when she thought their hiding place had been compromised. She was an attentive mother.

The second pregnancy ended in the birth of a single kitten that didn't survive the first six weeks. Born weak and never really able to walk, the little female may have been injured inside her mother as Malya fought so violently with the wild hog that damaged her eye.

She stayed with the dead kitten for days, licking it incessantly. Her final act was to consume it.

Early life for Steed and Tally had been typical, and in one aspect, quite amazing. Shortly after birth, both were able to maintain body heat for two days. That permitted Malya to be gone up to 36 hours, traveling as much as 5 miles a day to find and return with food.

Their eyes opened normally on the 12th day. At about 15 days, they began to walk. In their 7th week, Steed and Tally were eating red meat.

At six-months, the spots on their coats began to fade, and the classic buff color developed. The kittens made their first kill together, a small spike buck, when they were less than 14-months-old.

For the cubs' first 14-months of life, Malya was not only cautious and caring; she was attentive to the small things they needed to know if both were to survive. She was conscientious in teaching life's lessons. In her balanced approach to parenting she was as ready to play as to scold.

But three weeks before she led her young on the grueling, off-the-cuff trip north, she'd grown quieter, less playful, and more vicious in the manner of her kills. Impulsive rage had come to characterize her acts of predation as much as an even-handed strategy to feed the family. The cubs began to question many of her actions and non-actions. The change in her personality was gradual but certain. A less cautious, more brazen, yet strangely withdrawn Malya was emerging.

>>><<<

On the morning following thc slaughter of the coyotes, Steed was doing what he'd done so many times before, rubbing his head against his mother's shoulder.

With a sudden snarl, Malya whirled in his direction, lowering her head and exposing her teeth. Her pupils were narrow and her ears laid back.

Steed quickly withdrew, moving back two steps. That wasn't far enough for his mother. She came to her feet and charged, driving Steed from the clearing where the cats had been resting.

Steed sprinted into the tree line. He was frightened and very confused. His mother had never treated him in such a way.

"Why do you chase, Steed? He did nothing wrong," asked Tally, still lying on the other side of the clearing.

Malya turned toward her daughter, and didn't stop the attack until two firm nips to Tally's hip sent the female hustling into the brush.

[191]

Both cubs stood still for several moments, not sure what to think or do.

"Mother, why are you chasing us away?" asked Steed. Just the inquiry was enough to bring Malya into the trees in his direction, growling a warning the meaning of which was clear – *it's time for you to go!*

Steed pedaled backwards hard, turned, and broke into a full run away from the two females he'd shared life with for almost two years. He didn't return.

Malya's next charge sent Tally running in the opposite direction, with her mother's snarling threats filling her ears. As with Steed, the meaning of Malya's actions was frightening, but clear – *go with your brother, and go now!*

Malya sat down at the spot from which she'd issued her final growl toward Tally.

There was a small voice that argued for the cubs to remain, while something equally deep inside insisted the cubs do what other panther cubs do.

As any mother might be, the she-cat was conflicted.

In recent days, in this new land, Malya had considered whether it would be better if she and the cubs remained together. She sensed they were the only ones of their kind in the new wilderness. There would be no more cubs born to Malya. She knew the same would prove true for her offspring. In the end, reason lost out to the centuries-old urges of instinct – as with her first litter, the cubs must make it on their own.

>>><<<

Malya had dealt with the first reality at hand – expelling her offspring. The second would be more personal, more drawn out than the decisive action she'd just taken.

Approaching nine years of age, Malya realized her health was failing. For months she'd known decisions proved more perplexing, once razor-edged skills were less sharp, and her temper more difficult to control. She tired more easily, and her breath seemed to shorten earlier in each day.

Malya hadn't told the cubs, but the vision in her left eye was completely gone.

Also, on two occasions she'd stumbled and experienced difficulty getting up. One day she struggled with dizziness and the next nausea or severe headaches. On really bad days, it was all three.

A life's worth of eating fish or mammals that fed on aquatic life, had loaded her body with mercury. The scattered tumors she carried were in their sixth month of growth.

Twenty-Four
Taking Mutton off the Menu

It was more than a skip and a jump from the lower end of Sumac Swamp to Ken and Rhonda Moon's place. In previous years the couple would see wild hogs only on a limited basis, mostly two or three coming over from Sanderson Slough. But in the summer of 1958, things changed. Sumac Swamp hogs began to make their way north to raid Ken's chicken coop, destroy nest boxes, eat eggs, and kill hens, all of which were eaten on the spot.

>>><<<

An attack in the late summer of '59 had been particularly destructive.

When it started, Percival was on the other side of the house, sleeping in his favorite spot under the corner of the barn. The damage was all but done when he finally heard the commotion and headed for the coop. At 10-years-of-age, the full-blooded Welsh corgi's hearing wasn't as keen as it used to be.

Like all members of his breed, Percival looked like he'd been slighted when the designer got to the part about legs – then tried to make up for it when he sketched in the ears. Whatever might be the contrast in proportions, Percival was tough as a pine knot, and committed to protecting Ken, Rhonda, the farm, and his owners' livestock.

His determined spirit is what earned him the name, "Percival" – a name he shared with a member of King Arthur's legendary Knights of the Round Table.

When he arrived at the trench under the chicken wire, barking, bouncing, and raising all manner of what for, the two sows bolted through the chicken wire to make their escape.

As was commonly the case when homeowners surveyed damage done by plundering hogs, Ken and Rhonda were amazed by the apparent ease with which the wire had been ripped from the horseshoe nails in the almost-new posts.

What was even more surprising was the resized hole in the wall where the chickens moved between the coop and fenced-in area. The sows gained access by simply caving in the planks around the foot-wide opening.

>>><<<

Chickens were one thing, but in the past year the Sumac hogs' interest in the Moon's place had taken a really bad turn. No longer were chickens the target; it had become Rhonda's sheep.

The long-time Basin residents had one of the largest flocks in South Carolina. They had chosen the Dorset Horned breed for two reasons – prolific lambing and meat. Managed properly, some ewes could produce as many as four lambs per calendar year.

Of course, there was wool to be had – extremely white, close, high-quality wool, free from dark fibers. But Rhonda's primary interest was in dollars generated by livestock sales, racks of lamb, and grilled mutton on weekends.

Serious predation pressure on the flock began when Wartek became aware of the consistently large number of lambs, and the tasty, delicate nature of the flesh. To slow and hopefully stop the swine caravans coming up from the Sumac in search of lamb and mutton, the Moons would have to deal with Wartek.

Ken and Rhonda, along with Max Mullinax and Samantha Wyatt, may have been the only people to have gotten a good look at the Sumac terror. In fact, several months back, Ken got a shot at the brute, barely missing when the slug passed just in front of Wartek's chest.

>>><<<

"You know what happened the last time we chased these young ones don't you Wartck? The Obtruders almost ended your days my big friend," said Ezy as he followed Wartek along the edge of Upper Mossy River.

Wartek didn't respond to Ezy's statement. As he often did, Wartek chose to let his thoughts rattle about only in his head.

But they didn't, did they Ezy? The thunder passed me by, and I enjoyed my second lamb of the day. I've learned what to do among the soft, white ones – how to remain beyond their horns, and escape with their young. I have no fear of the animals or the Obtruders. No one does it like me.

When it came to the big, rust-colored hog with the irregular black spots, there was only one word to describe his self-regard – "boundless"!

Ezy continued to express his uncertainty about Wartek's intentions. "What are we going to do if both of those rams are in the smallest pen? They're both as bad as they come. The smaller pen you're talking about makes it easier for us to corner a lamb, but it also makes it easier for the rams to corner us."

"And what about the dog without legs? He's small, but his bites are painful, and his barks never end. If he brings the Obtruders, this time their gun may find its mark!"

"Surely, you worry about that, Wartek?"

"There's a difference in worry and caution, Ezy. Besides, I don't have to worry. I have you to do that for both of us."

>>><<<

Were Wartek to worry, it would likely have been more about the two large, aggressive rams than Percival's bluster and short-range nips, or even Ken Moon's rifle. A shot would have to be taken from a distance, in the dark, and at a moving target. The threat posed by the rams was fully "in your face". Clearly, for Wartek, the meat of tender young lambs was worth the risk.

The entire Moon flock was horned, but the horns on the two dominant rams' headgear were heavy-duty and shaped to deliver nasty wounds.

On each, particularly on Slammer, the final 6-inches tended to point straight out rather than roll back into a circle. It made for two sharp spikes that were potentially as dangerous as any boar's tusks.

>>><<<

That day there were two kinds of news – good and could-be-worse. As hoped, a large group

[198]

of sheep, including a number of lambs, were in the smaller enclosure. Also, the loosened bottom strand of wire on the fence where the hogs entered had not been repaired. That was the good news.

The could-be-worse news was that only one of the bruising rams was among the group – Slammer, the older, larger, and more aggressive of the two. Slammer was the one that looked more like a small Charolais bull than a Dorset sheep. There was the hump at the back of his head, thick legs, a power-packed neck, and strikingly-broad, muscular confirmation. Even faced off against Wartek, he was quite a brute in his own right.

Ezy followed Wartek under the bottom strand of wire. Feeling uncertain about the whole thing, the smaller, younger boar seemed to feel as though staying close to Wartek would keep something bad from happening. And, if it did happen, being in the shadow of Wartek's great confidence might somehow help him escape the worst of it.

Both assumptions would be proven wrong!

There was no strategy in place. The plan was simply to charge, panic, and separate one or more lambs from the ewes. The two hogs would then respond to Slammer according to how Slammer responded to them.

The Sumac delegation might well have benefited from more of a strategy – not that a more cautious or informed approach would have made much difference.

As the chase started, one ewe and two young lambs broke off from the flock. Wartek was quickly after the closest lamb. Ezy managed to pin an undersized yearling 15-feet from where Wartek was chasing the lamb. The remainder of the flock scattered toward the upper end of the lot.

The sheep's baas, the bleating lambs and the grunts of the two killers brought Percival running toward the lower pen. His full-power pace showed with every dip in his long back between two pairs of absurdly-short legs – his stomach seeming to drag the ground with every bound. Every tooth in his upper jaw was gleaming.

When Percival reached Ezy's left side, his distraught threats were enough to turn Wartek's sidekick away from the dying sheep. Ezy charged the Corgi, barely missing with the upward thrust of his tusks. The stumpy dog ran in circles around the large black hog, managing to score a bite on Ezy's right rear leg.

Wartek paused briefly from pulling upward on mouthfuls of flesh and entrails to watch Ezy confront Percival. His head shuffled thoughts typical of his detached attitude.

Ezy...kill the dog with no legs. You can surely overcome such a small opponent. At least occupy him, so I can eat what you have left.

With Wartek's back turned as he continued to dismember the lamb, and Ezy occupied with Percival's lunging attacks, neither boar saw the farm's top ram coming.

Slammer's race toward the two boars threw his younger cohort into a fit inside the gate to a nearby pen. Hammer had been separated from the flock while a tear in the flesh of his cloven hoof healed. Smaller than Slammer, the younger ram was no less willing to defend the flock.

That day Slammer needed no help!

Thwarted in his earliest attempts to rout wild hogs, Slammer had grown more capable and determined to strike a decisive blow. The ram accelerated as he neared Ezy, exploding into the hog's side. The base drum sound of the lick testified to the power Slammer was able to generate in a running start of less than 20-yards.

Ezy was knocked a foot into the air, and 10-feet across the narrow flats at the southern end of the enclosure.

As the Sumac hog bounced and skidded to a stop on his left side, every protective impulse in the powerful ram's body urged him to stay after the boar. The final blows were delivered from above. The sharp tips of Slammer's horns pierced connective tissue and broke ribs as he twice stood on his hind legs, and dove into Ezy with all the power his muscular frame could muster.

Following that first horrific blow, Wartek had abandoned the half-eaten lamb and trotted several yards across the gentle slope from the spot where Slammer was pummeling Ezy.

Even the Sumac's fiercest warrior was rattled by the fury Slammer demonstrated in his attack. Somewhat stymied on an occasion or two in the past, not until that day, had Wartek witnessed the huge ram's full fury. For the first time in his life, the overriding impulse felt by Wartek was to flee.

Seeking to further express his rage, Slammer spread his front legs and raised his head, partially lifting Ezy into the air. That's when something completely unexpected happened.

[202]

Two ewes crashed into the downed hog, the first fracturing Ezy's eye socket, and the second cracking Ezy's skull. The ram's rage proved contagious.

In a remorseless finale, Slammer stood on his hind legs a third time, swelled his chest, and drove both horn tips into Ezy's neck.

>>><<<

As the final death blows were struck, the Basin's biggest bully was pushing his way under the fence and heading back into the woods. Once under the barbed wire, Wartek didn't turn south toward the Sumac. Rather he headed north in the direction of Sanderson Slough.

There was no real rationale for the Sanderson option. It was just that...even Wartek couldn't quite bring himself to desert his companion and run straight for home.

He spent the evening in and near the cool water of Sanderson, trying to stop the bleeding from the long cut on his back received while hurrying his great bulk under the sharp wire barbs.

For the first time, the bruiser's reckless disregard had been just that – too reckless and too dismissive of the facts, resulting in the death of his most devoted companion.

[203]

Twenty-Five
Wartek's Fall Reprieve

Through the fall and into the early winter of 1960, the Hunt Club didn't really launch another dog-led hunt for Wartek.

Members' interests were directed more toward whitetails, turkey, coons, doves, quail, and the two out-of-state trips. Throw in the holidays, and there was always something that conflicted with a second large-scale hunt in the "Wartek War".

Instead, *"y'all keep an eye open for the beast"* became the maxim before every weekend hunt. He had by no means been forgotten. That would be difficult to do with his picture posted on the wall in every high-traffic area in the building.

Member Nick Mitchell's daughter, Sissy, was quite an artist, and it was she that drew the Wartek-wanted poster.

Member bets were everywhere as to which one would get the boar. Wagers ran the gamut from a simple $20 bill to the looser paying to have the hog shoulder-mounted for display in a place of the winner's choosing.

On the main bulletin board there was also a letter from Samantha Wyatt, expressing her appreciation for the club's plans to do away with the boar that caused her so much suffering.

Any plans for legal action by her family had been dropped. Samantha had visited the hunting lodge on a couple of occasions. She continued to be a lover of the outdoors, and was comfortable being in the company of people who enjoyed the forest. She'd also been a hunter most of her life.

The odds of anyone collecting on a bet as to who would take down Wartek were far slimmer than any of the hunters realized. He had left Sumac Swamp, and appeared to have found a new home in the Basin's northern-most slough.

Sanderson was considerably smaller than Sumac, but the wet areas were just as wet; the mud just as inviting; the sows no less receptive, and the hunting equally promising.

Or, so Wartek thought.

Twenty-Six
And That Changes Everything

Six weeks pasted, and Thorn still refused to condone Renshaw's full admission into the Thicket Pack. The short-haired pointer hunted and ate with the group, but full acceptance had not been granted.

The holdup was simple – Thorn didn't like the thicket's newest arrival. But events lay ahead that would change things for many of the Shady River Basin animals.

>>><<<

It was a crisp, fall afternoon. Nolton and Thorn were scenting the northern-most edge of the territory. Laps around the perimeter usually fell to Corvin and Nolton, but that day Corvin was hunting muskrats with Chesman. Thorn joined the bear-dog on the northern swing.

For several minutes, the two had trotted along without exchanging a word when Nolton broke the silence.

"Thorn, many of us remain perplexed as to why you are so easily angered by Renshaw. He seems like a good enough sort."

"I'm not angry at him. I'm just not at ease when he's around. He's not like us. His breeding is pure, and his ways are not those of the deep woods," replied Thorn.

"Would he fight hard to protect our home? Does he have instincts required to kill quickly and cleanly? I can't help feeling he would prove weak at both. I believe our group would be better served if the place he wants is kept for another."

Thorn was not being truthful, and Nolton knew it. His response was unspoken, but his thoughts were clear.

Thorn, you're only kidding yourself, as you seek to mislead me. My question is a lot more honest than your answer. The truth is, you don't like Renshaw because he is very different from you.

Nolton and other Thicket Pack members could see Thorn was natured very differently from Renshaw. Thorn was inclined toward conflict, and Renshaw toward communication – Thorn toward aggression, and Renshaw toward accommodation.

[208]

The Pack leader had touched upon the crux of the issue when he mentioned Renshaw's breeding. The pointer was what Thorn could never be – something that distressed the Rottweiler daily. Thorn's father had been a bully and a killer, and Renshaw's an admired and skilled champion among the Obtruders.

Thorn was dealing with the reality that there are traits to be valued other than overpowering force, even in the deep woods. In the simplest terms, the leader's discomfort with Renshaw was nothing more than intimidation with a splash of envy thrown in for good measure.

>>><<<

With Novic and Chesman pursuing muskrats and Novic sleeping atop the monolith, Renshaw took the opportunity to move toward Izepha's side.

She was well into her second month of pregnancy. There would be pups in less than four weeks.

Gwenfar was sitting outside the great rock, watching as Renshaw spoke softly to her good friend.

"I hope you feel well Izepha."

"Good Renshaw…I'm feeling good."

Their relationship started in keeping with the dictates of nature. No courtship, no romance, no fanciful love affair had preceded their union. But something out of the ordinary had developed

[209]

between the two, something deeper than was typically found in a feral relationship.

Somehow Izepha sensed this newcomer from the Out World was different – less detached, less brutish than other Thicket Pack males. Almost from the beginning she was strongly attracted to Renshaw. But what was truly unique about the elegant pointer in the world of feral males was his abiding interest in remaining with Izepha. His attraction to her far exceeded the moments involved in their first union.

"Soon, the others will see Gwenfar's brother is not the father of these pups. We have not spoken about this, and it's something we must do," said Izepha.

"What are your thoughts, Renshaw? Do you think we should stay and deal with what is to come, or do you think we should slip away?"

Her direct, serious-minded approach to things was very much part of what attracted Renshaw to the female. She was smart, and her demeanor more refined than typically found in deep forest ferals.

"We will not be slipping away, Izepha. You, the pups and I will need more than I alone can provide. We must stay here and face what each day brings."

"I would like to ask you something. Has Chesman shown interest in the coming litter? Has he asked questions about how you feel or what he can do to help? I've not seen or heard him do so."

"No, he's asked no questions, and shown little interest in the coming births. He is so disinterested I believe he's failed to realize there is no way this litter could be his."

Renshaw turned and looked directly into Izepha's face. It was something he'd never considered.

"No way they could be his...you mean...?"

"I mean... there is no way they could be his. The pups can only be yours Renshaw...only yours."

If Chesman was that removed from the fact and circumstance of Izepha's pregnancy, it could be the coming revelation would prove less disruptive than Renshaw had previously feared.

There was comfort in that thought, given Renshaw's broader interests.

But, regardless of how things were to go upon the pups' arrival, the strong, long-muscled pointer with the red head and neck, was prepared to deal with Chesman and Thorn. His comparatively mild-mannered nature was not to be confused with trepidation.

In his deepest, most private thoughts, unknown even to Izepha, Renshaw's plans were more encompassing than dealing with Chesman.

Thorn had no idea what he faced in this new rival from the Out World. Renshaw wanted more than a sheltering rock over his head; he wanted to lead the Pack.

>>><<<

Only yards from where Thorn and Nolton planned to make their turn back toward the den, the Ross' youngest basset hound arrived on the other side of the Lower Mossy. As best he could, Zero was jumping and barking. The three rolls of extra skin piled up around the year-old basset's neck, and the two rolls above his stumpy knees served to make jumping a task.

Both Thicket Pack ferals stopped and watched the stubby defender of Ross property put on his come-and-get-some-of-this show across the river. Both were prepared to ignore the hubbub, until Zero's father showed up.

Multiply Zero's dimensions by a factor of 2.5 and you have a mental picture of Double Zero. Much larger and louder, his contribution to the cross-the-creek challenge proved more than Thorn and Nolton could take. Both headed across the stream to take on the now-retreating white and brown hounds.

Over any significant distance, the bassets stood no chance of outrunning the massive ferals. But their head start grew as Thorn and Nolton were slowed by the Lower Mossy's stout current.

It may have been the lingering irritation from the earlier discussion about Renshaw; the simple fact he decided to teach the clumsy-looking house pets a lesson; or nothing more than his pervasive mean streak taking over that ignited the angry pursuit of the hounds.

Thorn meant to do them more than a little harm, and the bassets knew it. Both were digging hard for the safety of the porch.

Realizing Zero and Double Zero were heading straight for the Ross' backyard; Nolton was ready to break off the chase long before Thorn. On a couple of occasions, the Thicket Pack had tangled with the owner's of the dairy farm. In fact, one of the newer members had been shot dead by Wilma Ross.

As the bassets entered the yard, still issuing assorted, throaty, barks, Thorn and Nolton slowed and came to a stop in the edge of the trees. Nolton was feeling increasing ill-at-ease with the reactionary pursuit of the bassets.

The story of Korson impulsively leading his group into the hunter's camp, and the devastation which resulted had become legend among the Thicket Pack. That was the image filling Nolton's mind as he and Thorn stood at the edge of the yard where the owners were known to be a threat.

>>><<<

"Thorn, let's go no further. These people are trouble. Forget the long-eared dogs," urged Nolton, just as the .308 slug ripped into the base of his neck. Neither dog saw Norvel Ross standing at the back corner of the house. Before they came to a stop, he had carefully placed the crosshairs on the lion-dog's upper chest. Ross applied the single pound of pressure necessary to fire his favorite rifle. Nolton's back bowed as the 180 grain bullet drove him backwards.

An instant after Nolton fell, Thorn made his second bad move in the past five minutes. Staying 15 feet inside the tree line, he ran to his left rather than turning back to flee in the direction from which he'd come.

His angle of flight took him deeper and deeper into the woods.

Only a few knew the hole was there, much less how long the rotting planks had been lying across the opening.

As it turned out, the decaying planks had been there plenty long enough to splinter under the weight of a large bounding dog.

The hole which took Thorn's life was dug by prisoners in the spring of 1901. It had been the source of water for inmates serving time at the county prison farm.

Many knew of the farm's existence and its reputation for housing the worst of the worst, but few if any knew of the three inmates' bodies that decades before had ended up at the bottom of the well.

Two died at the hands of other prisoners and the third at the bidding of a corrupt and vindictive warden. It was the disappearance of the third inmate that prompted the current warden to order another well dug only two years after the first had been completed.

The low, rough-hewn lumber bunkhouse building burned down in 1911.

As the camp's physical remains had dissolved back into the Musclewood, so had remembrance of the hungry hole and the secrets it held.

The hand-dug well was 35-feet deep and almost 4-feet wide, with 7 feet of water waiting at the bottom.

After bouncing repeatedly from one side to the other, Thorn went head first into the dark-green, stagnant muck.

With his great power, Thorn, yelping and whining, managed to struggle back to the surface four times before disappearing for good.

All that remained were the raking, marks on the dirt wall, where Thorn fought desperately for life. Even for a dog with such a violent and regrettable past, such a death seemed unfortunate.

In less time than it took for the water at the bottom of the well to again grow still, that day's events served to redirect canine lives in the Basin for years to come.

Twenty-Seven

Advantage Renshaw

From time to time, animals in the deep Musclewood Forest would leave the den on what was to be a routine mission, never to return again. But the disappearance of Thorn and Nolton, on the same day, was more than out of the ordinary.

It was Gwenfar and her brother, Chesman, that were burdened most by the mystery of the two's disappearance. They were the only ones to make any serious attempt to find some answers. Even with them, the efforts consisted more of random trips along the northern edge of the territory than elements of a serious search.

Thorn's treatment of Gwenfar had been only slightly less inconsiderate than for other Pack members. She was not heartbroken. However, she couldn't help being troubled by not knowing the fate that had befallen her partner of several years. It remained a question to which she'd never have an answer.

Norvel Ross used his small track hoe to dig the hole into which he dumped and covered Nolton's body. Neither Norvel nor his wife ever knew about the bottom of the well serving as Thorn's final resting place.

>>><<<

In his planning to take over, Renshaw couldn't have anticipated anything more to his advantage than the events at Ross dairy farm – the two biggest obstacles to his plan had been removed.

Following Thorn's disappearance, the inevitable leadership vacuum quickly formed.

By default, Renshaw soon became an unquestioned member of the Pack. His two competitors for the role of dominant male were less than formidable.

Novic was too passive to assert himself in a serious leadership competition. Chesman was equally ill-suited to take over Thorn's role. He was smaller and less intelligent than Renshaw. His low, rumpled build made him look older than his years. No member, including Chesman himself, doubted he would subordinate himself to the German pointer. In addition, the new developments meant Renshaw having sired Izepha's pups would not prove to be a distraction.

[218]

Within ten days of the deaths at the Ross dairy farm, Renshaw's following consisted of Novic, Chesman, Gwenfar, and Izepha – two below-average males and two females, one pregnant. It was hardly the makeup of a strong feral pack, planning to dominate the future. As had Thorn before him, Renshaw was facing the challenge of future-focused leadership of the Thicket Pack.

>>><<<

However, Renshaw had little concern for the specifics of pack make-up. It was not his intent to return to the old power-broker days.

During his time in the thicket, he'd seen many clashes involving deep woods animals, including two particularly bloody skirmishes with members of the Sandy Knoll Pack.

In one fight, Thicket Pack members attacked a young Carolina Dog, badly mauling and ultimately killing her. She was heavily-pregnant at the time. Her desperation-filled efforts to get back to her feet and the safety of her den stuck with Renshaw.

He was determined to find a better way for its creatures to share the Musclewood Forest – a way that would serve to insure longer lives for the young, including thc pups hc and Izcpha wcre awaiting.

Twenty-Eight

The Chicken House Campaign

Steed and Tally's response to being expelled by their mother was very atypical. Of course, for the young cats almost everything had been out of the ordinary for the past four months. Rather than splitting up and going their separate ways, the brother and sister remained together.

The shock of Malya's action and the strangeness of their new home drew them closer together and strengthened their bond. How long the sense of co-dependency and mutual commitment would last remained to be seen.

Tally would become sexually mature before her brother, and the chemical changes in her body would go one of two ways – complete rejection of Steed or inbreeding. Either way, what lay ahead was a dead end.

Shortly after leaving Malya, the siblings selected a warm, dry spot in a compact area of palmetto as a resting place. It was located northwest of No-Toes Thompson's house, 2-miles above the junction where the Upper Mossy ran into Shady River.

Except when hunting, they stayed near the den. On hunting forays they most often went together, but at times alone. When either made a solo kill, at least a portion of the prey was brought back to the den. It was something their mother had imprinted on the two from an early age.

>>><<<

The chicken house campaign – their most trying and noteworthy hunt – started well after eleven o'clock on a rainy Wednesday night. The coastal plain for miles in all directions had been drenched by a late-evening rain. In hopes the thunder and lightning would ease off, the cats delayed leaving the palmetto cover for almost three hours.

"Steed, I'm trying to decide if the noise in my ears or the rolling sound in my stomach is louder.

[221]

How much longer before we can hunt without worrying about the storm? I'm very hungry!"

Steed looked one more time at the sky and then at the puddles standing in all the pathways leading out of the palmetto. Tally had always spoken her mind, but in the fundamentals of daily decisions, Steed took the lead. The decision as to when they would depart was his to make.

"It looks like much of the storm has passed, Tally. Come on. Let's hunt."

No consideration had been given to a specific hunting spot or prey they would seek. The only requirement was that whatever they killed must be large enough to feed them both, and feed them well. Steed took the lead, choosing a path that led Tally along Shady River toward the Lower Mossy River intersection.

He was heading for an area where they'd hunted twice before. On their first attempt, they took a medium-sized hog, and on the Panthers' second effort they caught two beavers away from their lodge. Tally handily killed the female, but the larger-than-average male managed to reach the edge of the pond.

Steed was right behind, when he latched on to the beaver's hard, flat tail. It took a few minutes, and more than a little effort to kill the 40-pound rodent. Steed ended up spending as much time avoiding the sharp, orange teeth as he did positioning a killing bite. He'd taken beaver before, and he knew the reddish-brown fur was soft to the touch. However, he was equally aware that a careless move could result in the loss of a sizeable plug of skin.

The two aquatic mammals made for a substantial meal. But that night they wanted something more substantial than beaver. Steed had venison on his mind. Not since the day they killed the coyotes and ate the doe their mother provided had they filled their stomachs with their preferred meat.

Steed knew it wouldn't be easy. It never was, especially when driving rain sends deer to ground beneath thick cover. Bedded down, it was all but impossible to stalk and ambush a healthy whitetail, even though the Florida panther was particularly well-equipped to do so.

Proportionally, the panther's back legs were the longest found on any of the big cats. It gave them their astounding ability to jump a city bus – long ways. They could leave a tree limb or other overhead perch, traveling great distances before their prey even knew they were in the air. But for the ambush technique to be most effective, prey animals needed to be up and on the move.

>>><<<

With just over a mile to go, Tally realized that Steed's destination was the dilapidated old building across Shady River from No-Toes Thompson's home.

[223]

The area in front of the old chicken house had been cleared, but the back was grown up with head-high bushes and vines. The back side of the roof on the falling-in structure was intact, permitting Steed to move almost 100 feet from one end to the other, surveying the undergrowth and inspecting the excellent hiding places it contained.

The chicken house was the place and rooftop observation the method he'd used to find and ambush the hog. That rainy night, he and Tally hoped to discover another large meal using the thick growth to escape the storm.

Steed got on the roof by jumping to the trunk of a tree, and then onto the corner of the building. Tally was right behind. Shifting into ultra-quiet mode, the cats sheathed their claws and began walking slowly along the edge of the tarpaper roof.

On the first pass, the siblings saw nothing of interest. Half way back, Steed stopped and eased down to his chest. He was studying the brush from his immediate left back to the corner where they had gotten onto the roof.

Keying off her brother, Tally turned around, dropped down, and began to again study the brush they'd just passed on the return trip. With only 50-feet of potential cover to monitor, it would be unlikely anything could enter or leave the growth behind the building without one or both cats seeing the movement.

Thirty minutes passed, and neither Panther had seen anything of interest.

Just after 2:00 AM, Tally opened her eyes. She'd been asleep for almost 45-minutes. The rain had stopped, and the lightening had moved away, becoming bright, thunderless flashes in the distance.

Surprised by the ease with which she'd dropped off to sleep, and a little embarrassed she'd fallen short in her duty, Tally was quick to whisper, "Steed, I see nothing in this direction. Have you seen anything?"

There was no response.

"Steed, have you seen any movement?"

The second, extended silence turned Tally in the direction of her brother. His head was lowered, and his front legs drawn up under his chest. He was in that unmistakable initial crouch of a predator. Another distant flash of lightening brought Steed to his feet, although still low and ridged.

The double flash that followed drew Tally's eyes to the mottled outline in the brush. A large buck was curled up under gnarled shrubs and vines.

Only moments before Tally awoke, the buck had gotten to its feet. Steed had managed to resist the impulse to launch an attack. It was fortunate the experienced hunter hesitated before making what would have proven a rushed and likely unsuccessful leap.

The great deer hadn't stood to leave its hiding place; rather it had stood to turn in a circle, paw the ground, and lay back down. The deer's movements served Steed's intentions. He was settled back to the ground, facing away from the two cats. Things looked more promising for a kill.

>>><<<

The pending encounter between Steed and the buck was not unlike most encounters between predator and prey. Understandably, most emotion turned in favor of the prey, particularly if the kill was grisly and violent.

The responding counsel offered by people who took a more objective view, usually went something like, *Oh, the predator has to eat too!*

That statement was true, but without doubt, there was something uniquely troubling about the rainy-night attack Steed was planning. Unknown to the Panthers, the target was Cashon, one of the most venerable deer to ever roam the Musclewood.

Cashon, always cautious and physically precise, had managed to live 12-years in the wild, a very rare achievement. He'd sired scores of young. His splendid bloodline was found throughout the Shady River Basin, and well beyond.

Cashon was that classic buck. He was the one that's seldom seen – a ghost, a phantom, an exaggeration, a real-life legend that's coveted by all hunters. That was the case with every member of the Shady River Hunting Club. There was agreement among the members that the iconic buck's shoulder-mount would go above the double doors leading into the dining hall. There he would confirm the club's hunting prowess, while speaking to the Basin's reputation as the home of outstanding trophy whitetails.

In years past, Cashon had escaped the water's-edge threat posed by alligators; any number of feral dog pursuits; one singularly harrowing attack by a large black bear; the flames of two Basin wildfires; and an assortment of hunter near-misses.

In the larger of the two fires, not only had Cashon saved his own life, but he'd managed to lead many other Musclewood animals to safety, including entire families. It was a feat which won him unending gratitude and enduring fame.

>>><<<

But, that night, at the back of the abandoned chicken house, slowed by age, Cashon faced the greatest threat of his life.

Steed didn't take his eyes off the well-concealed buck as he whispered to his sister. "Tally, go back to the other end of the roof...get to the ground...come around to this end, and be prepared to help when I jump."

Tally's movements were fluid. The pads on her feet shunned sound as the female appeared to float across the roof, around the front of the building, and back to the rear corner.

Things went as planned until the moment Tally looked slowly around that back corner.

It may have been that she'd made the slightest sound getting into position; perhaps, as she crossed in front of the building, the breeze carried her scent through the open sides to the resting deer, or it may have simply been that Cashon's still-keen senses picked up something. Somehow he knew things just weren't right, as he'd known in so many critical moments before.

Steed watched as the great buck rocked up on his rear legs, and then to the front, before snapping his head from side to side. There was every indication he was about to flee.

Steed's plan to get closer by moving slowly along the edge of the roof quickly evaporated. There would be no time for a stealthy, distance-narrowing approach. Tally's brother wanted to land far enough up Cashon's back for his jaws to reach the top of the deer's neck. There he could sink his teeth into the backbone at the bottom of the skull.

Steed knew well the advantages to be had in killing prey quickly, especially one the size of Cashon. Skill or simple luck, a well-placed tine had killed many predators.

Steed's quick interpretation of Cashon's movements was correct. Often he'd seen whitetails detect a threat, stiffen and snap to attention.

Just looking at Cashon, his breadth and maturity, Steed understood how wary the buck must have become over the years in order to reach such physical stature.

The cat's thoughts quickened, and his muscles grew taut as the moment of decision neared. The harmonized tension of predator and prey was classic.

Steed took two powerful strides before the great springs that were his rear legs drove him into the air. But as he feared, the short running start and resulting 25-foot leap failed to put his jaws above the targeted place on Cashon's neck.

His forelegs and claws only reached the large buck's hips. Cashon lunged toward open ground. Steed slid off the deer's left hip as Cashon powered his way through the undergrowth.

As she'd done at the county landfill chasing the deer, Tally was coming from an angle on the right, hoping to head off the buck. Distracted by the cat clinging to his left side, Cashon didn't change his direction, and Tally's projected point of impact was exactly where she found the Musclewood legend's right shoulder.

Steed's sister threw both left legs over Cashon's back, sinking her claws into his left side. On the right, her front claws were pulled into the shoulder muscle, while the right rear nails dug into the soft tissue at the waist. The aging deer, slipping into a deepening state of shock, didn't fully feel the claws as they sunk into his flesh. Instinctively, he focused on running, running as hard as he could.

As Tally grappled to get her teeth into Cashon's neck, he made a sharp, powerful turn to the right. Steed was slung off, crashing through several bushes as he tumbled away from the chase.

The 220-pound buck was the largest Tally and Steed had ever challenged. Even at 12-years-of-age, his muscles were firm, his frame wide, and his determination to escape, as strong as ever.

With Steed no longer pulling him down from behind, Cashon picked up speed, stampeding past a sizable Sabal Palm tree. As he intended, the thick knobby trunk swatted Tally from his side, sending her rolling across the cocklebur-filled sand. It was a predator-shedding tactic Cashon had used before.

For a moment, Tally lay unconscious. When she came to, the mixture of numbness and pain ran from her right jaw to her right rear leg. She'd taken a hard lick – one that took her out of the contest.

Even though he'd managed to shed both cats, the wise, old deer knew things were looking grim. He'd never encountered felines like the two he faced on that stormy night. He'd never dealt with such power and speed. There would be no outrunning them.

Cashon spun and turned his twelve points in Steed's direction. Bleeding and falling into even deeper shock, Cashon decided to stand and fight, rather than risk another running attack from both sides.

Steed skidded to a stop, and began a circling motion to Cashon's right. The revered buck slowly rotated, always keeping the sharp points of his rack between himself and the cat.

[231]

As Steed circled, his thoughts sparked.

His neck, I need to get beyond his defense and find his neck. If I can do that, I can kill him!

The first attempt came as Cashon briefly took his eyes off his nemesis. Steed charged Cashon's right shoulder. The charge was low and powerful, but all he succeeded in doing was to discover just how valiant the old buck still was.

The sharp point at the end of Cashon's right main beam gouged the soft tissue under Steed's chin. The Panther threw his head into the air and rolled off the top of the buck's antler. The pain flared from his head to the bottom of his shoulders. The antler had provided a reality-check for the young, highly-aggressive cat. Cashon was still a very dangerous animal.

Not until his fourth, more-cautious attempt, did Steed manage to get his teeth beyond the cluster of sharp points. He wrapped his front legs around Cashon's neck, and bit as hard as he could just behind the buck's lower jaw. From that point on, Steed confronted Cashon's next defensive tactic – raising his rear leg as high as possible, and driving a sharp, cloven hoof into Steed's side.

Almost ten minutes of throttling and dodging were required for Steed to arrive at the obvious conclusion – Cashon's broad throat was too wide and muscular for him to cut off the volume of air moving through the buck's windpipe.

A different ending-strategy was called for.

It took five more minutes and twice as many attempts for Steed to accomplish his new objective – getting his jaws over Cashon's nose. There, the leverage he exerted was several-fold what had been possible when he was biting at the whitetail's broad, muscular throat.

With the cat's mouth covering his entire muzzle, Cashon managed to land three more painful kicks to Steed's ribcage. Two were primarily glancing blows, but the third was so direct and deep it almost cost Steed his grip on the deer's muzzle, not to mention his own consciousness.

Not until the bone, cartilage and other connective tissue within the nasal passage caved in did Cashon stop kicking.

Well before it came, the heroic deer knew the end was at hand.

Steed maintained his bite, suffocating and ultimately confirming Cashon's death.

>>><<<

After releasing his grip, getting to his feet, and giving his head and shoulders a good shake, Steed headed straight for his sister. She was sitting up, but had not stood since the tree trunk batted her to the ground.

"Tally, your leg is bleeding, and your eye is closed."

[233]

"My eye and right side hurt badly, Steed. I hope I never am hit like that again. Do you think all my parts still work?"

It was a serious question, asked in an amusing way. Steed's reaction was to nuzzle his sister's neck.

"I sure hope they do. If you can, please stand and we'll see," replied her brother, giving his sister additional licks once she got to her feet.

It was dawn before Tally was confident all her moving parts were in fact still doing what they were designed to do. Fierce soreness had already set in. Ten days would be required for her eye to return to normal.

>>><<<

For the next three days, while recuperating and consuming the deer, a rear corner in the chicken house became a temporary resting place.

The morning of the second day the Panthers remained close to protect their kill. Steed was sleeping in their chosen corner, and Tally was resting on the roof of the poultry house when she noticed a column of buzzards circling on the far side of Shady River.

With plenty to eat hidden in the brush below, and her ability to travel hindered by bruised and painful muscles, Tally chose not to investigate.

It was a fortunate choice.

[234]

The large black birds were spiraling down toward the deflated, rust-colored carcass of a once-magnificent cat, whose only surrender had come to an insidious invader, against which she had no defense.

Twenty-Nine
Holiday Happenings on the Knoll

As New Year's Day, 1961, approached in the Out World, two developments altered life among the Carolina Dogs on the Knoll. Seph and Bedwyr's pups arrived, and Mace had disappeared.

The 4-week-old litter consisted of two females and one male. All three were healthy and handsome, displaying the earliest signs of the erect ears and tightly-curled tail which distinguished the Carolina Dog.

Both females were the exemplary buckskin color worn by so many individuals within the breed. But the male, from head to toe, was a rich gingerroot red. The striking coloration came from deep in his father's lineage.

While the new arrivals were celebrated, the disappearance of Mace remained a dark cloud over the Knoll, particularly for his half brother. Corvin had never heard nor seen Mace give any indication he was unhappy or would consider leaving on his own. Carolina Dogs were gregarious. They coveted companionship and understood the benefits of pack life.

None of the Pack believed Mace vanished on his own. On one occasion, Corvin summarized the group's thoughts while drinking at the edge of a Shady River tributary with Gaius, Enid and Bree.

"Mace is experienced. He knows the dangers in the forest. I've got to feel there's still hope he will return."

Corvin was right, and Corvin was wrong.

Mace could indeed handle most threats found in the deepest parts of the Musclewood, or in the most threatening parts of the Sumac Swamp, but not all.

>>><<<

The indiscriminate snare at the edge of the Sumac's deepest water was intended to restrain, not kill. Avery Melmon would do the killing.

The long-time trapper's unforgiving wire worked with Mace. It held the Carolina Dog for almost a day before the 11-foot American alligator saw him. Unfortunately, for all but the alligator, the crusty old trapper only had to clear the noose of Mace's lower leg.

Avery did so while muttering his usual sentiments when cleaning up after one of the large reptiles.

"No 'count, thievin' gators!"

>>><<<

Life and death were anchor events in the lives of Sandy Knoll ferals, as they were in the life's story of all deep woods creatures. But sometimes it was the less dramatic, less evident moments that foretold a sea change.

Two weeks later, such a moment came when Enid and Bree were playing with Bren, Banner, Modred and Castle near the edge of Shady River. The pups, at 16-months, had taken what used to be cavorting and turned it into something more akin to roughhousing.

Enid and Bree were taking a second break when Enid noticed a dog watching from a distance.

[237]

Its red head was raised, and its overall posture erect and attentive. The dog's stare was fixed, but its manner showed no sign of threat.

The onlooker was Renshaw. For the first time, a key Thicket Pack member had approached Sandy Knoll without bad intentions.

Issuing two soft, inquisitive barks, Enid trotted a few yards in the direction of the visitor, where he sat and returned the German pointer's scrutiny. There were no follow-up barks from Enid.

Instead, there were only inquiring looks exchanged by two historical foes.

Thirty

A Field Trip w/ Commentary

No better argument could be made against judging a book by its cover than Raford "No-Toes" Thompson. From his bibbed overalls to his well-worn brogans, his look and pace were those of a plodding work horse, but his brain was pure thoroughbred.

He'd farmed most of his adult life, only taking time out in his late twenties to complete work on a degree in biology, with an emphasis on mammalian embryology.

He'd always felt detailed study of the origin and growth of an embryo was key to understanding the fundamentals of living organisms. He'd also found time to complete half the hours required toward earning a Master's Degree in the narrowly-focused field of study.

Those who knew him well understood his fascination with wildlife came more from personal passion than pages in a text book. In his mid-fifties, it turned out he'd much rather pet a young beaver or raccoon than leaf through the pages of a biology text on aquatic mammalian evolution.

Since his wife's death, Raford had divided his time between raising soybeans, teaching part-time at a small church-affiliated college, big-time gardening and his favorite avocation, experiencing the Basin's wildlife.

Not only did No-Toes like to observe, he took every opportunity to tell others about wonders to be discovered in the deep woods. That's how he met Rory and Alenna Laws. He was leading a field trip for the youth group at Shady River Baptist Church, where the Laws family was active. Once since then, he'd taken Rory and his sister to the lower end of the Sumac where he knew otters were active.

Rory, Alenna, and Raford had come to enjoy each other's company. The Laws' children helped fill a long-standing void in Raford's life. He and his wife had been unable to have children of their own.

The kid's liked the shiny gold watch chain hanging across the bib of No-Toes' overalls, as well as his deep barrel-chested laugh. Conversely, Raford enjoyed the kid's light-hearted laughter, and their inquisitive minds.

>>><<<

At the breakfast table on the Sunday following the day of otter-watching, Rory and Alenna could hardly contain themselves as they

[240]

told their parents about the river otters' antics and Raford Thompson's running commentary.

"Dad, he knew all about how long they live, what other animals they were related to, how trappers nearly killed all of them, what they eat, and what other animals try to eat them," said Rory.

'Mom, he said the babies are called pups, and they didn't even open their eyes for a month. The mother otter must have her hands full if they can't see for so long," added Alenna.

"Yeah sister, but Mr. Thompson also said the babies stop drinking milk after three months, and are gone off on their own after six months. Mom and dad got us for a lot longer than that, Alenna. They got it worse than that mother otter," inserted Rory, seeming to offer clarification he felt his sister's words required.

It earned him a brief, reprimanding look from his mother, before she turned to look at her husband.

Murray and Ellen smiled at one another, delighted with the quality experience Raford had provided their two oldest children.

Obviously, at 2-years-old, Robbie couldn't stay quiet or still long enough to join his brother and sister on a field trip. But his time was coming.

Following the meal, Ellen asked about something she'd often wondered. "By the way honey, do you know why they call Mr. Thompson,

[241]

"No-Toes"?" asked Ellen as she began stacking dirty dishes.

"I'll tell you about that a little later."

Her husband didn't want to get into the subject with the children listening.

It was 9:30 before Murray and Ellen were able to sit down and relax by the rock fireplace.

After an almost simultaneous sigh, Ellen asked the question again, in a single word.

"Well?"

"Well what?" responded her husband, lifting his head from the headrest of his favorite over-stuffed chair.

"Why do they call Raford Thompson, No-Toes?"

"Okay. The story is, when he was a boy working in the pasture with his father, his feet slid off the axle of the tractor. Before his father could get things shut down, both feet got under the front of the bush hog. The blade went through his boots, cutting off his left big toe and the entire front of his right foot."

"They said if it hadn't been for his daddy tying Raford's belt around the calf on his right leg and the sleeve from his own shirt around Raford's left ankle, the boy would have bled to death before they could get him to the hospital."

[242]

Ellen shook her head as she stared into the fireplace.

"As active as he is, he has obviously gotten beyond that handicap."

"No kidding! Folks at the Club say one of his favorite sayings is: "There's more to me than my scars!"

>>><<<

It took a full day and Raford Thompson's farm truck for he, Rory, and Alenna to get the job done, but Rory's metal hunting stand was no longer behind the house. The three deep-woods explorers took a day to move it to the southern end of Sumac Swamp.

The reason was simple; that's where the beavers were. Raford knew of an active colony, and the elevated platform would make the beaver-watching much easier. Three cushions, some binoculars, a canteen of water, several candy bars and another field trip got underway.

Beavers held a special interest for the biologist-turned-farmer. Around the turn of the century, intense trapping pressure had almost killed off the population around Shady River, as well as the much larger Savannah River Basin.

In 1940, six beavers from Georgia had been reintroduced into the area by specialists from the U.S. Fish and Wildlife Service. Over the next 20 years more beavers from Georgia were found to have migrated into the drainage area. The large, luxuriously-furred animals had managed to make a comeback.

In the Sumac colony, a monogamous pair, their two most recent kits, and one female from a previous litter were making their home in a lodge at the edge of a pond excavated by a resident pair two years earlier.

Raford kept his voice down as the youngsters leaned in, hanging on every whispered word. The beavers were out and active, moving gracefully through the water and waddling about in their familiar, ungainly manner.

Raford missed nothing as he described the life and times of North America's largest rodent:

...their impressive size, with the largest males sometimes reaching forty pounds;

...webbed rear feet used to swim;

...nimble fingers for spinning limbs and sticks while bark was stripped away, corn-on-the-cob style;

...the hairless, flat tail used as a danger signal in the water and a leaning post when sitting on land;

...the long, incisors which grew throughout the animal's life and served to reach the nutritious cambium layer under the bark;

...the multi-level design of the lodge, with a drying and eating platform just inside the underwater entrance, and a drier, much neater upper level where the family slept;

...their preference for woody plants such as willows, birch, maple and poplar;

...the beaver's willingness to travel miles in search of soybean fields, where they cut the entire plant off at the ground, and drug it back to the stream to use in constructing dams;

...the second set of lips behind the teeth which closed when the animal dove;

...the valved ears and nose, and, of course,

...the fur coat comprised of soft, downy underfur and long guard hairs.

It was great stuff for two intelligent, inquiring children.

Field trips didn't get much better than sitting in a hunting stand, watching a beaver family cut and gather plants for the underwater larder, while a larger-than-life narrator sat at your side explaining each motive and corresponding action.

>>><<<

Two hours after the threesome's arrival, the afternoon light had begun to fade. It was time to head home.

Had Raford written a script for the afternoon, couldn't have been any better? But that special day, the Musclewood was about to double down on the afternoon's experience.

[245]

All three had gotten down from the stand, and started for the truck when Alenna brought things to an abrupt halt.

"Hey, look over there!" she shouted, grabbing her brother's arm and pointing toward the water's edge. Roby jerked his head in quick, side-to-side motions trying to focus on what had caught his sister's eye. And then, there it was.

A short distance across a narrow cove off the main pond was a scene destined to become a life-long memory for the Laws children, and a certain addition to Thompson's list of great stories from the forest.

The kid's chaperone-narrator had seen many things in the Musclewood: clashes between remarkable birds of prey; the fox that managed to climb well into a tree to get at the baby crows nested there, and the two bobcats that joined forces to take down his neighbor's young bull.

But the scene across the pond would rank among the most unusual and intriguing in Thompson's quiver of yarns. He had many stories to share, and that one would become one of his favorites,

Thompson was no less transfixed by the scene than his young partners. After a brief pause, he began a narrative which became his most inspired of the day – by far!

[246]

"You know guys, watching an otter play it's easy to forget just what ferocious predators they really are. They are kissin' cousins with badgers, and you know what tough critters they are."

"Look at his long body and flattened head. That streamlined shape helps him slip smoothly through the water."

"Most folks who find the otter particularly interesting believe they are among the smartest of all furred creatures. And they're probably correct in that belief."

"They're fun to watch, but you wouldn't want to take them lightly. They're killers - far more vicious than they look when frolicking in the water."

Raford raised the binoculars, and there it was; a large river otter pumping oxygen in and out of widely-flared nostrils. There was good reason the 4-foot male was breathing heavily through his nose. His mouth was full of tough hide at the back of a 5-foot alligator's neck.

The children stood close as Raford dropped to one knee. Adrenalin was pumping, and Raford's creative thought processes were racing. *Look at that...incredible...large fish, eggs and small mammals, okay....but an alligator?*

>>><<<

After all three had used the binoculars, the children really cranked up – each question filled with excitement.

"Mr. Thompson, do you think the otter can kill an alligator that big?" asked Alenna.

Raford's "biologist juices" were churning, as he looked for a little scientific weight to put behind his interpretation of the real, swamp-life drama. His reply was by no means off-the-wall. To the contrary, his analysis likely held a great deal of truth.

"Well, kids, now that the otter has gotten it out of the water and up on the land, he has a real advantage over that 'gator. I believe his plan is simply to wear the alligator out. Alligators are quick and strong, but for only short periods of time. They get tired real quick."

Rory was next. "I don't see how the otter's teeth would be long enough to kill that alligator Mr. Thompson. Do you?" His question got to one No-Toe's was already turning over in his head.

Now that he's got it, how in the world is he gonna kill it?

As Raford continued to watch through the binoculars, he began to formulate another, even more interesting theory.

"You know what son, I don't think the otter's gonna have to use his teeth to kill that 'gator. I believe Mother Nature may just do that for him."

"You see, as the 'gator tires, and like I said, he'll do that quickly, his muscles fill with acid, and just stop working. Then the otter can concentrate on a spot where his bites can best get through the thick skin. Once he's into the meat, he can do some real damage."

"It's the lactic acid build-up in his body that's gonna do that 'gator in," said No-Toes, as he continued to follow events through the binoculars' lens.

When Rory finally got the glasses again, he could see places on the back of the alligator's neck where strips of skin and flesh had indeed been stripped away.

[249]

In another 15 minutes, the 30-pound otter had been joined by to other members of the bevy. All were soon eating freely – the alligator likely still alive, but deeply in shock.

>>><<<

From the daily lives of North America's largest, most elegantly-dressed rodent, to a highly-unlikely predatory event, it was the kind of thing Raford Thompson most enjoyed – animals showcasing their lives in customary, as well as unexpected ways.

Thirty-One

Izepha is the First to Know

The Thicket Pack had never seen anything like Renshaw. His array of personal qualities was seldom, if ever, found in a deep forest feral. The reason was simple; the rangy German pointer wasn't one.

Like the true feral dog, he wasn't two or three generations removed from Obtruders and the socialization influences of the Out World. He had known their care and concern, watching as they knelt to make sick or broken animals well. Renshaw understood not all Obtruders intended the deep woods and its creatures harm.

Running ahead of a well-practiced hunter; responding to crisply-shouted commands; joining an equally-artistic companion on point; and enjoying the thoughtful treatment of an appreciative breeder; had shown him what living in harmony with other creatures, even Obtruders, could mean.

His intellect had been sharpened, and his general upbringing influenced by the company of other animals of championship lineage. He thought before he spoke, and stood ready to defend positions he took. He had been shaped by more than the struggles of life in the deep woods.

If anything, the trials he'd known since escaping from his abusive second owner had only served to further round out his character and strengthened his determination to promote a more tolerant life among the Basin's animals.

>>><<<

Renshaw had given the matter much thought. The evening had come in which he would share his thinking with Izepha. He sat nearby, waiting for her to finish feeding their four, 3-week-old pups.

Long a stabilizing presence in the Pack, Izepha was like Renshaw in her elegance. She was only one generation removed from pure-bred spaniel status.

Before moving close to her, Renshaw watched warmly as she licked the final pup still drawing on one of her front teats. He'd always found her movements to be sensitive and compelling. He was pleased by many of her traits, ranging from her manner in motherhood to the careful deliberation shown when considering options for the Pack's future. He genuinely wanted her counsel, and hopefully her concurrence.

Renshaw sat just behind his mate as one-by-one the babies fell asleep. Izepha continued to lick two of the sleeping pups as Renshaw began.

"Izepha, I love our young, and will always do what I feel is best for them and you. I hope you have confidence in that," said Renshaw in a near whisper.

"Certainly I do, Renshaw."

"My time in the thicket and experience with past warring is limited. But I have seen the damage it can do, and the lives it can cripple and cut short. I don't want you, our pups, or others in the group to live each day under the threat of violence."

Izepha raised and partially turned her head back toward Renshaw. As usual, there was no quick response, only a moment of obvious reflection. When her response came it was in the form of a question.

"What's on your heart, Renshaw?"

"I plan to make contact with the Sandy Knoll leader about a more peaceful future."

Another moment of silence passed, in which she pushed up onto her haunches, and turned completely in Renshaw's direction.

"Violence has always come with life in the Basin. It is forced upon us and required of us. To find peace with the Sandy Knoll leader is one consideration, to coax it from all who have grown up facing years of Thicket Pack aggression would be a far more complicated task. This would certainly be true with the father whose son was recently attached and killed by Thorn."

"Unknown to you, I have observed the Sandy Knoll Pack on three occasions, and I am sure the father and his mate have new young. Perhaps the fire in their heart has been quenched by the love they feel for the new pups. As you know better than most, Izepha, where love is, anger often can find no room."

"What will Novic and Chesman say about your intentions?"

"I will handle those two."

"....and Gwenfar?"

"Gwenfar is like you; she is clear-thinking and wiser than most. She will support my actions. That can be assured, if you and Gwenfar continue your friendship and you talk to her about supporting me."

"Please, don't interpret my words as weakness or fear. If forced, I will fight to the death

[254]

to defend the lives of our young and the Thicket Pack home. But as long as I lead, it will be in the direction of a future less threatened by the violence that grows where no understanding is found."

Thirty-Two
Missing the Good Old Days

As Renshaw planned for a hopeful future, Wartek longed for the past. He missed pasted times in the Sumac where his strength and threats intimidated so many, so easily, so often.

Since the night Slammer and the angry ewes killed Ezy and he arrived in Sanderson Slough, Wartek had known nothing but frustration. The Sumac heavyweight had come to know two things for sure – he was not the only bully in the upper Basin, and returning to the bad-boy-life without the benefit of a well-established reputation was no simple trick.

First, and foremost, there had been the issue of food. In the Sumac, he'd found and held sway at all the best places. But in the Slough, a new array of eating places had to be established.

Even though wild hogs would and could eat virtually any plant and animal available, they still had to find places where the odds of a decent meal were in their favor. From eggs to amphibians, catfish to carrion, Wartek scoured the Slough and surrounding homesteads for places where he could eat – not only eat, but eat in peace.

"Eat in peace" was the key notion as Wartek worked the area. At each foraging place he'd found, there were always others which strongly objected to his presence.

At one of the best places to uncover abundant roughage there was a family of foxes. The close proximity of their den inspired a constant, pesky assault on Wartek. The male, female, and both nearly-grown kits made his grubbing all but impossible, with their unabated darting about, their nips and endless yapping. Their busy-bee assaults were bad enough, but the heavy, musty smell they and their den emitted made eating at that choice spot even more trying.

>>><<<

In many places, it was other hogs which led the protest, noisily staging fake charges to discourage Wartek.

One challenge he faced was more than exaggerated, noisy bluster. Nepling and Vife meant every word they said, and every belligerent act they undertook.

There were acorns, fruit, seeds, nuts, bark, roots and frost-toughened mushrooms to be grubbed. There were hatchlings, small mammals, birds, as well as small reptiles which could be killed and eaten, but it all came with the persistent threat posed by two of the Slough's most cantankerous boars.

The brothers were three years younger than Wartek, but their combined bulk and combative nature matched or surpassed that of the Sumac immigrant.

The first time Wartek encountered the brothers, he had taken an aging cat from its owner's yard. Sleeping in a straw laundry basket, there was no time for the cat to react before Wartek used his snout to pin the yellow tabby against the

[257]

bottom of the basket and drive a tusk through both shoulders.

As he carried the body toward the woods, Nepling advanced from the left and Vife from the right. It took less than a minute for the brothers to rob Wartek of his prize. Many times following the loss of the cat, the boars were successful in chasing Wartek away from a good rooting spot or a choice piece of carrion.

Together, always together, Vife and Nepling were like no other wild hog challenge Wartek had encountered. For the first time in his life, he felt repeated impulses to turn and flee when the Sanderson duo launched their 45-degree, simultaneous charges toward his flanks.

On one occasion, he stood his ground, pushing and stabbing at the boar brothers with his formidable tusks. It was his best effort, an effort which had always proven sufficient in the past, but against the belligerent Sanderson Slough pair he was able to no more than hold his own.

Two months up north, and he was more than ready to return to the friendlier confines of the Sumac.

Thirty-Three

A Wise Old Bird

Captain wasn't the only deep woods predator Aster had seen fall victim to one of the Sumac's deadliest holes, only the most recent. Near the base of his favorite tree, the soaked, rotting vegetation which took Captain was thicker and hungrier than most to be found in the Sumac.

The loblolly pine preferred by the great horned owl not only provided a view of drama around the muskeg, but its tall, slimmer form afforded the opportunity to sit near the top and look across the treetops. From there, for many years, Aster had watched surrounding bird activity in order to locate nests, and the hatchlings they often contained. Once the target tree was spotted, he spread his 4-foot wings, and a kill was all but certain.

The raptor was in his 18th year, well into *old age* for his species. He'd lost his life-long mate in the previous year to a teenager's 12-gauge. The lost tested him, greatly! They had raised many owlets over the years – the majority in the same confiscated hawk's nest in a nearby tree.

Most creatures in the area agreed, the woods were poorer for having lost the highs and lows of their nightly love songs.

For a good portion of his life, Aster had embodied a curious if not unlikely blend of two things – the merciless impulses of a ruthless predator, and the patient insights of a Shady River Basin sage.

During the first 12-to-15-years of his life no small mammal or bird was safe in his 3-square-mile territory. Rabbits, woodchucks, bats, weasels, squirrels, possums, mice, a long list of songbirds, and even skunks were on the menu. He'd also taken herons, ducks, and a near flock of Canadian geese. On three occasions, red-tail hawks were killed and eaten – one in recent months.

But in his later years, Aster had become known more for his prudent counsel than his dogged predation. He'd grown to prefer mantling rodents on solid ground over engaging other birds of prey in daring, on-the-wing duels.

[260]

As he'd aged, Aster had literally moved lower in the tree, showing more willingness to engage his Musclewood neighbors. His day was more likely to involve good counsel than sudden death.

Even his look had become more that of the wise than the wicked. The tufted, ear-like feathers on the top of his head and the layered feathers on his legs and feet looked softer, more hair-like. His head looked as though it sat lower on his shoulders. His eyes seemed wider, a deeper yellow, more penetrating, as their gaze was dictated by the slow movement of his head.

Aster particularly enjoyed his exchanges with the Basin's larger predators – predators like himself.

Over the years, he'd shared the experience of returning to a family with nothing for the young to eat; the threat of armed Obtruders; the efforts of a determined, ground-dwelling predator to reach the nest and the young it contained; the loss of something precious; the scourge of the bad times, and the renewal of the good. Aster could speak thoughtfully of life's collective demands and the inevitability of death.

As with Enid and Renshaw, he was beyond experience, beyond skill, beyond smart. Aster was *deep-woods wise.*

>>><<<

Renshaw had never spoken to the renowned great horned owl. Only once had they been close

[261]

enough to acknowledge one another. Months earlier, as Renshaw walked by an old barn just off State Route 1102, he noticed Aster standing in the open loft door. The owl's evening meal was handing over the bottom edge of the opening. Fearsome talons on his left foot had insured there would be no escape.

The smell at the barn was almost caustic. Renshaw, whose nose was highly-tuned anyway, shook his head, more than once.

Renshaw slowed, as his eyes confirmed the message forwarded by his nose. Shortly before Renshaw passed by, Aster had cornered an eastern spotted skunk in one of the stalls. After the skunk succeeded in scampering up what remained of the barn loft ladder, Aster flew out the wide bottom door, circled, and soared back in the loft opening, trapping his target against the back wall.

The young black and white skunk couldn't know the barn was a favorite hunting spot. The great horned owl was one of the few predators on earth to routinely hunt and eat skunks.

Aster was just before flying away when Renshaw walked by, and tossed his head back – a gesture acknowledging both the owl's presence and prestige.

The great bird lowered its head, and sequentially rippled the toes on its right foot along the bottom of the opening. The pointer's nod and Aster's two-gesture reply was the only exchange between the two prior to Renshaw's visit. That day at the barn, the grand owl's strong sense of presence, reputation for discerning counsel and pure magnetism were what prompted Renshaw to pursue a visit.

>>><<<

As the Thicket Pack leader approached the loblolly pine, Aster was nowhere to be seen. A quick survey of the nest and limbs in a neighboring pignut hickory also failed to reveal the spot where Aster was sitting.

Renshaw sat and waited several minutes before deciding to head back toward Sandy Knoll. As he turned, he saw Aster in a graceful, shallow, descending glide through the trees toward the lower part of the loblolly pine.

The magnificent bird powered back, landed, and took the two deliberate steps necessary to turn on his favorite limb before engage the ratchet-like locking mechanism in the bony structure of his feet. The locking technique permitted Aster to stay comfortably atop the limb without constantly exerting leg muscles while facing Renshaw.

The German pointer had already settled back on his rump, studying the form of the long-famous Musclewood luminary. The Thicket Pack leader was no lightweight, but an element of what made him special was a willingness to accept being enamored of the grand bird.

The face was broad and studious, the eyes mesmerizing. The feathers looked as though an artist had airbrushed just the right blend of muted white and medium charcoal before adding a hint of soft tan and sea foam. Renshaw couldn't help focusing on the 5-inch talons that had so often stilled prey on the first strike, each driven into the victim's flesh by 500 pounds of pressure.

Passing each other at the bottom of the limb, the talon tips bore only one missing splinter of keratin on the middle finger of the left foot. Other than the single blemish, the daggers looked as polished and ready as ever.

The grand owl's use of a perch was precise. Smoothed over time by the raspy pads on his feet, the spot on the limb where he sat was narrower than the width of his chest. There were two worn spots further up the pine – one on a limb midwayup and another near the top. The three worn places implied his preference in limbs followed his interest in conversation. The higher his interest in a chat, the closer he sat to the ground.

There were two other indications of just how often Aster chose to return to the same limb. Only an eye as sharp Renshaw's would have quickly detected the clues.

The first was the horizontal scar across the tree trunk to the right of Aster's head, where he used a side-to-side motion to clean his downward-facing, scissor-like beak. The second was the weathered scattering of bones 15-feet below, where scant remains of countless kills had fallen and melded with the damp, decaying humus.

>>><<<

"You are from the Thicket and we have seen each other before," asserted Aster.

"Yes, I am….and, we have."

"Where is the big brown dog that leads your group?"

"He no longer leads. Thorn is gone."

Aster raised his head and thereby his eyes.

"Gone as in replaced or gone as in dead?"

[265]

"I belief the answer is gone as in dead. He went to the northern edge of our territory and didn't return. Both Thorn and the lion-dog are no longer in the thicket."

"They were together when they were lost?"

"Yes. They had left the den to walk the northern edge of our territory and never returned."

"You can know the Obtruders were involved. There is no likelihood that two of your kind would go missing in a single day without involvement by those from the Out World."

Aster paused a moment before speaking again.

"And what do they call you?"

"My name is Renshaw."

"Do you lead the Thicket Pack now?"

"Yes. With Thorn gone, I am leading the group. Our numbers are not as great as in the past, but it's my intention to make our future greater."

The owl abruptly ruffled his feathers, resetting the warm, insulating air between his body and the downy under layer. He again lowered his head to fix the huge yellow eyes on Renshaw, an obvious "please continue" gesture.

"Aster, I have come to speak with you about a plan, which many may question. But I feel strongly such an attempt should be made."

[266]

"….an attempt to what, my new friend?"

"I intend to meet with the Sandy Knoll leader about a more peaceful relationship between our Packs, and I am hopeful he will help make it happen. Do you know him?"

"I've seen him many times, but we've never spoken. I have on three occasions watched the Pack from the tree that shelters their den. All looks to be well. They have a large group."

Aster looked off into the woods, and the pointer continued to focus on the great owl's face. Renshaw sensed the feathered counselor was tooling his thoughts.

"It's unlikely the Sandy Knoll leader could lead without vision, or the ability to understand the link between choices and consequences. Also, there is no reason to think he loves his young or hopes for long life any less than you. I would think the best of him, before I expected the worst."

The venerable bird continued to stare into the woods, as still and mysterious-looking as pure thought itself. He raised his broad face, swallowed and adjusted the lower beak within the upper beak's socket. Finally, he spoke again.

"Renshaw, you must first convince the Knoll Pack leader of your sincerity, something I have no problem hearing in your words, and seeing in your eyes. It is something you can likely do. Then, most importantly, you must help him feel your idea is

[267]

his idea. The owl that sits beside you, making your favorite perch his own, will not saw the limb off beneath you!"

Without returning his gaze to the pointer, Aster continued.

"Renshaw, you and the Sandy Knoll leader coming together is the beginning. Staying together will be progress and working together will be the measure of success."

Continuing to look into the woods, Aster straightened his back, extended his neck, and rose to his fullest height. He was about to offer final words. In his advanced years, he no longer held knocking birds from the air or transfixing small animals with 4-inch talons to be among life's most satisfying things.

He'd become much more attuned to the feelings and struggles of other creatures in the forest. It was his new perspective that led the Musclewood mentor to solve a mystery that had haunted loving parents for many painful months. In his advanced years, it was precisely the sort of thing that brought him satisfaction.

"When you come to know the dogs on the Knoll, find the parents that lost a female newborn in the early morning hours outside the den – the parents I saw search so hard, so long. Tell them the hawk that took the small dog will be taking no more pups."

[268]

Aster then rode his powerful wings to another of his favorite limbs – the one near the top of the loblolly. Clearly, the meeting was over.

Thirty-Four
And Then There Was Steed

In addition to goats, Clinton and Peggy Dunlap raised tobacco and peanuts. Robert, their oldest son's farm was a few miles from his parents, where he worked three large tracts of soybeans.

The Dunlap name had long been associated with quality farming in the Shady River Basin.

On that Saturday morning, the job at hand would not take them to the fields. Clint and Robert were going to finish putting a new tin roof on one of the tobacco barns. As always, things got started before dawn with breakfast.

>>><<<

After filling a platter with scrambled eggs, Peggy stepped to the living room with her usual announcement: "It's ready and waitin'!" The percolator had quit growling, and the coffee was piping hot – just the way Clinton liked it.

Bob's dad was notorious for pouring the steaming brew into his saucer, blowing softly across the surface once or twice, and drinking it down – the blacker and hotter, the better.

Clinton followed three slurps with an exaggerated "aaaah", before glancing over at his son.

"Robert, anything's possible with enough coffee!"

It was a proclamation he'd heard more than once, but it still brought a smile to Robert's face as he looked across the table at his father's inflated grin. Breakfast was one of their favorite times of day.

Following scrambled eggs, fresh tenderloin and a bowl of Peggy's cooked apples, Clinton stepped back into the sitting room, and switched on the porch light. The yellow bulb was small, but it was about to play a role in the biggest fright of Peggy Dunlap's life.

All the hunters, farmers, and naturalists that frequented the Basin had their favorite stories about life in the Musclewood. Most were true, others less so. Peggy Dunlap was moments away from having one that would rank among the very best.

After turning on the front door light, Clinton glanced at the separation between the side curtains on the front door window. It was a good fifty yards away, but his sense was something had moved out near the barn. He pulled the right curtain back and moved closer to the square glass at the top of the door. The recently-installed pole light did a good job illuminating things around the barn.

"What ya lookin' at, dad?" asked Robert as he walked back into the sitting room from the back of the house.

"I'm not sure," said Clinton, reaching in his shirt pocket for his glasses.

Robert stepped to his father's shoulder, and pulled the left curtain panel back. Both men saw the same thing at the same time. It took several blinks, but things cleared up for the older Dunlap first.

[271]

"Land sakes, it's a blasted mountain lion," shouted Robert's father, as he reflexively stepped back from the window.

Robert's eyes confirmed the same thing, but his movement was in the opposite direction – toward the small square window pane. Making out exactly what was happening was made more difficult by 6-inch boards of the pen fence. Parts of the action were blocked from the men's view.

"I think you're right dad. That's exactly what it is, a dad-blamed mountain lion, and it looks like it's killed one of your goats!"

Had the Dunlaps prepared a list of things they expected to start their day, a mountain lion dragging the remains of a black and white nanny around in the yard would hardly have made the list.

"Can you believe that?" asked Robert, in what was clearly a rhetorical question. As much as anything, the initial reaction was a bolt of pure disbelief.

>>><<<

The nanny had actually been killed by Tally. Twenty minutes earlier she'd easily leaped the fence, landing almost squarely astride of the young goat. Steed joined her in the attack. The kill was quick and quiet.

As both cats opened the carcass and began to eat, lights in the Ross' kitchen window caught Tally's eye. More inquisitive than her brother, she

[272]

kept pausing to look up toward the house as she ate. During one other visit to the goat farm, she'd been tempted to take a closer look.

Steed knew exactly what was on his sister's mind and he didn't like it. "Tally, let's finish this meal and get back to the woods. Forget about going up there. You're asking for trouble."

Tally turned to look at her brother. She paused before beginning again to chew the muscle meat. In a rare, defiant moment, she turned her head again toward the Dunlap farm house.

"Did you hear me?" asked Steed, obviously becoming agitated with his sister's failure to respond and her almost unnatural fascination with lights in the window and the movements beyond.

"It will be okay, Steed. Don't worry. I just want to take a closer look. I'll be careful. Nothing's going to happen."

Steed reacted angrily. "Okay, just go ahead, but if you get in trouble don't look for me to help!"

Steed's anger was based far more on fear for his sister's well-being than on her failure to do as he'd asked. He genuinely didn't feel good about the whole scene. Killing and eating fully in the glow of the large pole light had put him on edge.

Tally knew her brother's concern was genuine, and she loved him for it. Her response came in the form of two extended licks on his neck and shoulder.

[273]

Steed struggled to restrain himself as his sister got to her feet and jumped over the pen fence for the second time. Including two pauses to look in several directions, the inquisitive Panther took a light-footed approach to the Ross' front porch.

Moving across open yard and easing around a Ford van, two pickup trucks and a tractor with hay rake attached was far removed from sheltering below palmetto plants in the deep Musclewood.

As edgy as the Panthers may have been, the shock and unlikeliness of the morning at the Ross household was about to escalate in an almost unthinkable way.

Peggy's scream was shrill and drawn-out, followed by the sound of her falling backwards against the kitchen table.

After placing a paw in each bottom corner of the kitchen window, Tally had lowered her face to within a few inches of the glass, just as Peggy looked up from the sink.

Strangely, Tally remained at the window when Clinton and Robert rushed into the room to see Peggy in the floor, holding on to the edge of the round, wooden table.

"Oh my God, what is it?" shouted Clinton, as he and Robert dropped to Peggy's side.

His wife could only point at the Panther's face, now slightly withdrawn from the glass.

[274]

Robert was the first to escape the shock that momentarily froze him and his father. He ran for the gun rack above the piano in the sitting room, where his father kept two shotguns and a 30-30 lever-action rifle. The Winchester in the top cradle was always kept loaded.

"Robert, be careful," urged Clinton, as his son pulled open the front door, and cautiously stepped onto the porch.

Tally was nowhere to be seen.

>>><<<

The sprint to the woods would have required covering quite a distance before Robert could get on the porch with loaded rifle in hand. Her instinct was to head up, not out.

Steed, still crouching near the nanny he and Tally killed earlier, watched as his sister jumped to the fuel oil tank beside the house, and then onto the flat roof of the recently-added washroom.

It was a risky move. Steed quickly realized retreating to the flat roof limited Tally's options to put distance between herself and the Obtruder moving around the house with the rifle.

Steed came to his feet and moved closer to the fence, lowering his head to look between the middle and bottom plank rails.

What are you doing Tally? Lay still, very still. If the Obtruder looks up, there may be no chance for escape. Why did I let you go near that place?!

Walking in a slight crouch, Robert Dunlap drew even with the metal fuel oil tank, less than 15 feet below the Panther. Drawing her upper lip to the gum line above her canines, Tally's inclination was to pounce. Lowering her head even lower, she chose not to.

Where did a mountain lion come from? No. It's got to be a panther, not a mountain lion. Many say panthers are in the low country...looks like they're right.

If it's under the house, it could charge out at my legs. But the house is too low for a cat that size...bet it ran around this side and headed for the

[276]

woods out back, thought Robert as he fashioned a series of images in his mind.

As her pursuer rounded the rear corner and stepped out of sight, Tally raised her head and looked toward Steed. Her brother was still standing just inside the fence near the barn. Filled with a sense of urgency, he reared up, and put his front paws on the top rail, permitting Tally to clearly see his head and shoulders.

They shared the same impulse – *It's time to break for the woods.*

>>><<<

Steed had easily cleared the wooden fence, and started for the trees just as the bullet sizzled by his sister's ear.

Clinton Dunlap was at the end of the porch with his .38 pistol.

Only Tally's slight turn in preparing to jump back to the ground saved her life. The second shot was equally close, sending the cat up onto the sloped roof, and across the back of the house.

At the far end, confused and frightened, Tally leaped for a tree.

In mid-flight, she hit severely-weathered power lines. The terrified cat bounced twice before the lines broke loose. Tally fell to the ground, enmeshed in the deadly, sparking coils.

While mercury contamination had slowly sucked the life from her mother, in an instant the

[277]

Obtruder's electricity hammered the life out of her daughter.

Steed raced for the deep woods, for the first time in his life deeply in shock and completely alone.

Thirty-Five
Sudden Satisfaction

The hot summer of 1960 seemed to moderate temperatures well into the winter months. By the time February arrived, there had been only two nights the Shady River Basin experienced a hard freeze.

By April, most seedling plants had emerged, as the coastal sun warmed the Basin floor. The early spring foraging was excellent, and the wild hogs were thriving.

Wartek had been back in Sumac Swamp for almost seven weeks. His old patterns were re-established, and the frustrations he experienced in Sanderson Slough were a fading memory. Little had changed during his absence. There were a few new faces, and several of the old ones were no longer around – victims of motor vehicles, hunter's rifles, and several instances of predation, especially with younger hogs falling victim to alligators.

On a pleasant day in March, 1961, Wartek was drawn to a spot just across Shady River from where Tanner Creek met the Shady's main flow. Two sexually receptive sows were making the fact widely known.

A third female, not in estrus, and three generations of young hogs joined the two receptive sows to make up the unusually large sounder. The group was foraging on the edge of a hammock clearing when Wartek broke into the open. His usual, exaggerated strut looked to be particularly well-tuned. The bruiser was feeling amorous.

>>><<<

Chances looked good for Wartek, with one exception – Roon. The black and white boar had

[279]

always resisted Wartek's strong-arm tactics, but had never opted to stand his ground in an eye-to-eye encounter. That day it would be different.

With grunts and posturing, it was Roon that started things. He was calling dibs on the two sows and showing a willingness to make it stick. Wartek immediately accepted the challenge, approaching his 4-year-younger and lighter opponent with a bristled-up, stiff-legged strut.

The silent, shoulder-to-shoulder pushing match began. Wartek was clearly larger and heavier, but Roon was younger, quicker and exceptionally strong.

Both animals slung their heads and tusks into the neck and shoulder of the other. Grunts and wounded squeals filled the air, as frothy, blood-tainted slobber began to cover both combatants. As was typical, each popped their jaws, and tried to come up under the opponent's head in hopes of getting tusks into the soft underside of the adversary's neck.

His eyes closed and his attacks beginning to show a frantic randomness, Roon had given about as much as he had taken, when suddenly, Wartek was no longer there.

It took a moment for the smaller boar to realize the horizontal swinging of his head was finding nothing but air.

The panicked dash for the trees made by hogs that had remained close to the fight did more to catch Roon's attention than the second crack of the rifle.

Roon fell in behind the shoats in running for cover. In a few seconds, there was nothing in the clearing but settling clouds of dust and the trembling body of the largest and meanest boar the Sumac had ever seen.

Wartek drove with his right legs, spinning in a half circle before drawing still. With a protracted exhale, he stiffened and threw his head back for the final time. Cheek muscles retreated in opposite directions, pulling his bottom jaws apart in a strange, twisted contortion. His eyes settled open, as a dust-filled haze began to form on the king boar's eyes.

Could it be that simple?

Could it be the observers who'd predicted a long, difficult and dangerous campaign were so profoundly wrong? Could the killer of so many competing predators and powerful hunting dogs be stilled in such a brief, unsuspecting moment?

The second shot from the .270 Winchester had torn into Wartek's chest only an inch to the left of the first round's point of entry.

The well-placed slugs brought to a close the nasty, protracted reign so many had predicted would last longer and prove far more difficult to end.

They were the first two shots at a wild hog taken by the hunting club's newest member, Samantha Wyatt.

Thirty-Six

And So It Begins

For Steed, the loss of Tally in such a sudden and disturbing way was beyond harrowing. He had no idea what strange force had knocked his sister from the air and jerked the life from her body.

For two days he retreated to the palmetto, and the depression in the ground he and Tally had shared. He dealt with his grief in silence, lying still for hours on end, seeking the few remaining whiffs of his sister's scent in the dried groundcover. It was only overpowering hunger on the evening of the third day that drove him from under the long, green leaves.

His still-disorganized thoughts were reflected in the randomness of his hunt. He moved south along the eastern side of Shady River, southwest of the Dunlap farm.

>>><<<

Steed had just crossed Dunlap Creek and entered the woods on the south side when Enid, Bren and Banner first saw him. The Carolina Dogs' initial impulse was to run. But the tentativeness in Steed's manner made them pause. His slight turn to the left away from the dogs struck the spark of pursuit.

Barking furiously, Enid's two 18-month-old sons charged, driving Steed back on his haunches. Enid, having faced down bobcats on more than one occasion, knew full well the power and speed that must be in the front legs of the much bigger cat. A single swipe, and one or both of the young males could suffer life-threatening injuries.

"Bren! You and Banner get back!" shouted Enid as he moved to position himself between his sons and the snarling cat. A quick movement

[283]

forward and Steed was able to catch the front of Enid's left shoulder with the longest claw on his right paw. The wound was superficial, but instantly bloody.

>>><<<

As they challenged the cat, Renshaw's first few barks weren't heard by the three Carolina Dogs. The German pointer was in a power sprint crossing Shady River. He was charging hard toward the barks coming from just inside the woods south of Dunlap Creek. He'd seen not only the confrontation begin, but the possible opportunity he sought.

Steed broke to his left when he saw Renshaw coming. Prior to reaching full speed, he ran over Banner, biting and clawing the youngster before breaking free.

While Renshaw and Bren sprinted after Steed, Enid moved to Banner. The wounds were in the meaty part of the shoulder. Banner would be stiff and sore, but barring infection the injuries should heal. Banner got to his feet, and tried to catch up with his father, who was 20-yards ahead in pursuit of Renshaw, Bren and the cat.

Seventy-five yards ahead, Steed dove for safety in the center of an entangled patch of briars and scrub oaks. Renshaw reached the edge of the undergrowth and skidded to a stop. He could see the Panther's wide yellow eyes and laid back ears,

[284]

both warning of bad things if the canids tried to enter the brushy entanglement.

Renshaw's hesitation was brief, before he undertook the contortions necessary to make his way through the thick cover. The pointer was drawing on his experience going after downed birds in places just like the one Steed had chosen.

Alternating whines and growls, it was clear the Thicket Pack leader had no intention of stopping in the face of Steed's threats and posturing. Not only was he coming, he was coming through the thickest part of the scrub brush. With the greatest opportunity for escape to his rear, Steed turned, and threaded his way out the back of the brush.

His next stop was 25-feet up a broad willow oak. The tree's lower, fork-filled configuration served to stop the dogs' pursuit. Settling near the top of the tree, panting vigorously, Steed decided to wait-out the ferals.

>>><<<

An hour after darkness fell, the dogs lost interest, and Steed was able to make good his escape. Before heading in opposite directions, Enid and Renshaw paused, holding their muzzles less than a foot apart. With only slight hesitation, Enid spoke first.

"Thank you for helping protect my sons."

[285]

Having long considered the dialogue he wished for, Renshaw's response put emphasis on the two leaders' mutual interests.

"As with many things, the cat is a threat to both our families. We surely have many shared interests."

The simple exchange would prove the beginning of a much larger and increasingly hopeful conversation.

www.ingramcontent.com/pod-product-compliance
Lightning Source LLC
Chambersburg PA
CBHW070306260626
47160CB00003B/744